A PONDERING HEART

REFLECTIONS: BOOK 1

SHARON HUGHSON

Expanded Edition © November 15, 2019

© Sharon L. Hughson in Portland, Oregon

Cover Art by Rachel543 on Fiverr

Editing by Lindsay Alexander

To all who believe and desire to know Him better
with thanks to the One who called and gifted me
and redeems all who come to Him by faith

PREFACE

Behind the Story

For several years, *Reflections from a Pondering Heart* brewed in my heart and mind. Sermons and study books stirred my creativity, keeping the idea of Mary's motherhood piping hot and ready to boil. And spill it did...onto the pages of this book.

Unlike other stories, this one isn't only a product of an overactive imagination. Yes, I've read between the lines and asked the writer's favorite questions: "what if?" and "why do you think?" In the end, I did my utmost to hold true to the Biblical recounting as given in the Gospels. After all, this is Mary's story to tell, and I hope she isn't disappointed with the authorial license I've taken in penning this journal.

Pondering Heart began to bubble over after multiple Christian women I respect made verbal observations about the mother of our Lord, Jesus Christ. The variety of ideas about Mary as a mother, a wife and a woman perplexed me.

Perhaps this awe of a woman who calls herself the Lord's Handmaid stems from her idolization by religion.

This "I could never be like that" mindset is too common among believers. This attitude haunts us and reveals a more serious issue. ***Contemporary Christ-followers believe Biblical people lived above sin and emotion.***

I know I've been guilty of this very thing. As a child, I remember learning about David and Goliath and thinking, "That's one brave kid." As in – he wasn't afraid of anything. But that's hardly the lesson scripture wanted to teach me.

Thanks to a lifetime of experience, I've learned a different perspective. Yes, David showed courage, but no one can prove he didn't fear the giant, or the army, or the king hunting him like a criminal. True courage pushes ahead in spite of fear, doubt, insecurities, uncertainties or any other emotional or physical stumbling block.

In short, David believed God was more powerful than all his enemies. He understood God's promises and trusted the Almighty to keep them. He knew an important truth we must grasp if we are to boldly serve the Lord:

Emotions are liars. God's Word is truth.

My Purpose in Writing This

Reflections from a Pondering Heart is a fictionalization. What do I mean by that? The story is based on actual events, but it isn't told as if it were a true story. The plot is expanded, adding drama and tension. I tried to keep my suppositions about Jesus' family life realistic to the times. This required a boatload of research.

My major sources for the information I used as a springboard: The Holy Bible KJV, Judaism 101 (at jewfaq.org), Holy Land Network.com, Biblical Chronology.com, Bible History Online, Cooking with the Bible.com, and Biblehub.com. Yes, I even searched images through Wikipedia.

I'm neither Bible scholar nor historian, but I am a woman trying to live for Christ in the 21st Century. Thus, I wrote this novella to give women hope. God has called me to encourage women of all ages with my writing. I pray this story will do that for everyone who reads it.

The Bible is meant to teach us and guide our lives. It is my conviction that in order to truly understand God's Word, we need to put it in context. What context am I referring to here? The people whose lives are recorded in the scriptures are human just like us. Grasping this reality in our hearts and minds will free us to serve our Lord with more confidence.

What this Story Isn't

This retold story is not intended to make any doctrinal statements. Neither is it an endorsement of a certain chronology. Argument exists over the actual calendar dates for some of the events attended within these pages. I needed a timeline, so I chose one. Thanks to my illustrious beta readers, I am not even including the calendar years on the journal's pages.

This story isn't meant to minimize Mary's important role in scripture. Mary is a holy woman who is to be admired. She is an outstanding example of what God wants a woman to be, but she was neither sinless nor perfect. She did, however, faithfully serve her Lord through some excruciating circumstances. After imagining living through these events hoping to lend authenticity to this recounting, I pray the Lord never asks me to endure anything similar.

The *REFLECTIONS* Series

What began as an "experiment" in self-publishing morphs into a series I'm highly unqualified to write.

Alas, God doesn't call the qualified. He qualifies the called. Especially in the area of fictionalizing true stories from His Holy Word.

This is the first book in a planned series of four biblical retellings. True stories from the changed hearts and lives of real women who lived and walked with Jesus Christ over two millennium ago.

I can only imagine what it was like to live in First Century Israel, but since imagination is part of my gifting from God, what better way to use it than bringing the Scriptures to life for others. Based on reviews from readers of an earlier edition of this story (one that had some typographical errors and fewer words), it's finding its mark.

Vicki from Wyoming says: "There are no words to sufficiently describe this BEAUTIFUL story. As a mother and a lover of my Lord - this book moved and touched me deeply."

Jessica says: "This book takes a brave look at Mary's life and shows the human side to her, bringing the reader into her world and her mind. I wish this was required reading for CCD classes! Not only was I drawn into Mary's story, her fears, her hopes, her dreams, I was amazed at the historical detail and the biblical accuracy as well. Highly recommended!"

My Invitation

Welcome to my time machine. Come inside with me. I'm setting the dials to the calendar year 7 BC. The location finder points directly to an insignificant village within the vast Roman Empire: a place called Nazareth, in the region of Galilee.

Close the hatch on your present-day world, and enter the Palestine of our Lord and Savior, Jesus Christ.

1

NAZARETH - CHESVAN

MY THIRTEENTH YEAR

*T*he day my world changed began like every other day in recent memory. An orange sun rose over the brushy hills. Pasty clouds chased each other across the blue expanse of sky. A refreshing chill from the autumn air nipped my cheeks.

I meandered along the worn dirt path. My destination was the same as every morning: the cave beneath the terraced hillside where my father planted his crops. Over the past three years, the path had worn to little more than a rut beneath the constant traffic of my sandal-clad feet and the goats' sharp hooves.

At the mouth of the cave, I swung the wooden gate toward myself and ducked to keep from knocking my forehead on the rocks. Not that I was tall, but the entrance wasn't even six spans[11] high.

When I entered our makeshift stable, the milk nanny rubbed her nose against the wool girdle that secured a water bladder to my hip. I pushed her away, scratching her forehead to ease the rebuke. She whined. One look at her engorged udder explained her urgent desire to follow me out of the pen. With one hand on her leather collar, I secured the gate behind me. Not a moment too soon. The other goats pressed their faces through the wide rungs. Their persistent baas echoed around the cave.

I patted a few of their heads. Pushing the shawl back onto my shoulders, I knelt to begin the task of milking. A hummed tune lifted my heart and kept the bleats of the kids in check. My thoughts wandered to the dream I had about my wedding last night. Rather than my face being hidden, the face of my groom was covered with a veil. Some say dreams have significance. If that's true, what did this one mean?

Soon, the udder hung limply, and the nanny pushed her nose into the enclosure. I never had to tie her as long as her kids were penned up. Most of the young ones were meat goats, not her babies at all, but she seemed to adopt them anyway. The goat knew mothering better than Anna, my father's wife. But I shouldn't complain. It would harden my spirit, and if my stepmother had taught me anything, it was that I didn't want to become bitter.

I carried the pot of milk through a narrow tunnel into a cool room. Light filtered through several fissures. I strained my eyes to make out the large pot and small jar sitting on a ledge in the wall. I placed the fresh milk beside the other containers and reached into the large pot.

The sour smell of curdling milk stung my nose. The curds were still too small and soft. At least one more day before the cheese would be ready for draining. One less thing on my list of responsibilities for today. I sighed. I loved making the cheese almost as much as eating it, but I hated listening to Anna complain about the smell when I brought it into the house to mix in the herbs and salt.

I scuttled back to the main cave, wiping my hands along my skirt. The goats bleated as I opened their enclosure. My little flock surrounded me, snuffling at my girdle, hoping for a treat. I laughed, fondling their ears while leading them into the scraggly grass surrounding our home. Now that the harvest was well past and Father's winter wheat plucked its head in the midfields, foraging became a chore. There wasn't much fodder, since they had been grazing these fields for a month. The time for selling the young ones neared. Luckily, the market for goat meat never waned in Nazareth.

With a critical gaze, I studied the three male kids. I would need to choose the most perfect one and keep it for Pesach[2ii], still four months away. Since I had begun caring for the goats, Father always let me decide which one was unblemished and fit for sacrifice.

Gamboling, frolicking, nipping at each other, the kids led the way to the watering hole. Adults pulled chunks of grass, wayward leaves on the bushes, and even strips of bark along the way. All around me, the pasture looked forlorn. It was nearly time to stake my herd closer to the house, where they would clean up the remainder of Anna's vegetable patch. Of course, I would need to be doubly certain she was finished with it. For such a small woman, her rants stung like a whip. At least she saved most of them for me or my sister, Mary (how confusing to have two Marys in the house), leaving my not-quite eight-year-old brother Jesse unscathed.

The sun rose, and my breath no longer misted in the cool air. I glanced at the sky, measuring the height of the sun. Still plenty of time to sweep the floors before Anna trekked to market, leaving me in charge of the young ones and preparing the midday meal for Father.

I herded the goats back into the cave, promising to give them another chance to graze before dinner. Maybe I was crazy for talking to them. They weren't human after all. But life could be lonely on a farm.

I pulled the jar of fresh milk from the cool room. Amazing how a single hour in the dark space dropped the temperature. I carried it in the crook of my elbow.

When I left the cave, a draft pushed the scents of goat, manure, and moldering straw away from me. I didn't mind the smell of the goats, but fresh morning air always relaxed me. My shoulders sagged, and I trudged away from the cliffs, never too anxious to return to Anna's domain.

As I rounded the bend, I glanced up at the dusty track leading to the house. What I saw froze me in place.

A most unusual man blocked the path. His white flowing robe reflected the sunlight. Golden-white hair haloed his sharp, pale features, which sparkled with iridescence. Eyes the color of the sky, seeming illumined from within, pierced me as easily as a sharp knife.

"Hail, thou that art highly favored."[3iii] His voice shook the ground. Or maybe that was just my legs trembling.

My heart thumped against my ribs, and my breath gurgled in my throat. I clenched the pot, unwilling to let my morning's work fall prey to my terror.

"The Lord is with thee," the man continued. "Blessed art thou among women."[4iv]

My mind spun, waking, at the strange greeting, from the paralysis his musical voice caused. How was a farmer's daughter highly favored? Certainly the dung caking the soles of my sandals sang a different tune. Who was this man to assure me of my relationship with Jehovah? Yes, I prayed each morning and night, as Father had taught us all, but how could this one know that?

Most disturbing was the final part of his greeting. Only one woman would be considered blessed among the daughters of Eve and Sarah. I was not that woman. I was just a girl.

"Fear not, Mary." He extended a pale hand toward me. "For thou hast found favor with God."[5v]

Was this a heavenly messenger? I loved Jehovah as much as any of my friends, but why would the Almighty give honor to a girl like me? A haze of unreality veiled my mind.

"And, behold, thou shalt conceive in thy womb, and bring forth a son, and shalt call his name Jesus."[6vi]

Now I knew the messenger had the wrong house. I couldn't have a baby, because I didn't have a husband. Yet. Was he accusing me of being intimate with a man? My face flushed.

"He shall be great, and shall be called the Son of the Highest: and the Lord God shall give unto him the throne of his father David."[7vii] I admit I gasped at this. "And he shall reign over the house of Jacob for ever; and of his kingdom there shall be no end."[8viii]

My stomach dropped to my feet, and my arm lost all

strength, sending the clay pot plummeting to the earth. It splattered near my toes, sloshing goat's milk onto the barren ground. The words proclaimed by this messenger echoed the prophecies of old and the promises made to my father's great-grandfather. The phrasing matched words spoken by my father's deep, warm voice during our evening devotions. A similar thrill evoked by those recitations tingled along my skin.

This messenger spoke of the Messiah, but what he said couldn't be true. I could prove it to him.

"How shall this be?" When I asked about this delicate subject, heat flooded my face, and I couldn't look directly at the man. "Seeing I know not a man?"[9][ix]

I was betrothed, yes, but I remained innocent. I might be a simple farm girl, but I knew how children were planted in a woman by the man's seed. And I had never been with any man in the intimate way reserved for married couples.

I pictured the kind face of my betrothed, and my heart skipped in my chest. He was godly, handsome even, but we had never even touched hands. To lie with him as a married woman? I couldn't imagine it.

The Lord's messenger didn't seem surprised by my question. He continued without pause.

"The Holy Ghost shall come upon thee, and the power of the Highest shall overshadow thee."[10][x]

A verse Father shared from the prophet Isaiah rang in my mind: "Therefore the Lord himself shall give you a sign; behold a virgin shall conceive, and bear a son, and shall call his name Immanuel."[11][xi]

My mouth dried like summer-parched ground. I forced saliva in, swallowing past the pomegranate in my throat.

"Immanuel?" It still came out as a whisper.

The angel-I can hardly believe Jehovah sent an angel to me-nodded and said, "That holy thing which shall be born of thee shall be called the Son of God."[12][xii]

My mind, whirling and bucking, refused to process the full meaning of these words. Even as I'm jotting the whole thing down now, it seems so unreal. A fantastic dream.

"Thy cousin, Elisabeth, she hath also conceived a son in her old age," the man in white said. "This is the sixth month with her, who was called barren."[13][xiii]

Elisabeth? She had been an old woman when last I saw her. Older than Father. Women that old were beyond child-bearing years.

The angel gave a slight nod of his head. He must have seen understanding glimmer in my eyes.

"With God nothing shall be impossible,"[14][xiv] he said.

Elisabeth had miraculously conceived. According to Jehovah's messenger, I would experience a similar conception. Similar, but not the same. The Spirit of God would father my child. My hand flew to my flat stomach. With fingers buried between the folds of my gray robe, I wondered how it would be possible. Had it already happened?

The man in glistening white garments waited. Did he expect me to have a return message? My throat constricted again. What could a poor girl say to the King of Glory?

Finally, I found my voice. It sounded stronger than I felt.

"Behold the handmaid of the Lord," I said, bowing my head toward the angel, "be it unto me according to thy word."[15][xv]

When I looked up, the path before me was empty. The

house was only a few steps away. My foot throbbed, waking me from my stupor. My smallest three toes had blackened ends. A puddle of thick white liquid slowly soaked into the ground.

Who can I tell about this? I can't tell Joseph. He would never believe such a tale. Who would?

ANNA HUFFED, arms crossed over her chest, when she shuffled down into the small room she shared with Father. Father and I had spent time together in the evenings since before my mother died. He taught me to read, write, and do sums. Some might accuse him of defying tradition (only men need these skills). However, teaching his daughter—who in turn taught her sisters—was a necessity. With all the labor required to keep the farm going, he didn't have energy for the record keeping.

I scanned the largest room in my father's house rather than looking him in the eye. I recalled all the hours of sitting here to eat with my family. I recalled sitting around the fire listening to Father's deep voice teach us the stories from the Torah. Now, the silence pressed against me like a weight. If I listened closely, I could hear my brothers whispering in their bed behind a hanging goatskin less than twelve spans away.

My father's hand patted my shoulder, and I turned my gaze toward him. Black eyes dwarfed the portion of his face not covered by his mostly gray beard. Heli bar Matthat, my father, concealed a host of emotions behind those dark eyes. I blinked to keep the tears stinging my own eyes from betraying how weak I really felt.

I knelt like a common servant at his feet, my hands clenched together. My heart felt lower than the hardened earth beneath my aching knees. He was sending me away to Elisabeth. I hadn't seen her in seven years. She came to care for Jesse after Mother died giving birth to him. Elisabeth, wife to a priest, had no children of her own and could be spared to spend several months with a widower and his three children until a more permanent caregiver could be found.

"I will arrange for you to travel with a merchant." Father's voice, low and gravelly, revealed what his face did not: disappointment, a hint of despair.

"Abba, I swear I'm telling the truth." I sounded like my youngest brother, Caleb, tattling on Jacob, who was closest to him in age.

Father's warm, calloused finger tilted my chin upward. The waning candlelight reflected off moisture in his eyes.

"I have always known you were special, Mary."

My lips trembled, smiling at his words. The tension gripping my heart loosened, making it easier to breathe. He believed in me. Warmth swelled my heart.

"You must not tell others," he said.

A knot twisted my stomach. Not tell others? But once my condition became evident, they would believe the worst about me. Did Father expect me to bear their judgments silently? Heat flooded my face as if I stood before an open flame.

"They will believe what they want," he said. "It is the nature of people to believe the worst. If you tell them . . ."

I watched his throat wobble beneath his whiskers. My shame would be his shame.

"Abba, no," I said, unable to keep a tear from streaking down my upturned face. "People will speak ill of you. I can't bear it."

"If I can bear their scorn, you can bear it." His harsh tone startled me. "We know the truth. Nothing anyone says will change it."

"But Joseph . . ."

Tears choked me. The thought of seeing pain in his gentle eyes raked across my soul. His opinion of me mattered almost as much as my father's. Joseph was older, but he had pursued me specifically, even though other girls had more appealing dowries. He would know we hadn't been together. He would think I had . . .

More heat flooded through my face and spread down my chest until I thought I might burst into flame.

"We will meet with him together," Father said. "I will explain your situation to him. Just the three of us."

"I'm sorry."

How could calloused hands be so gentle? He pulled me up, holding me on his lap as he often did with the young ones. I couldn't remember the last time I was held this way. Safe, for the moment, in his arms.

"Never be sorry when Jehovah's plans are not your own." His warm breath, smelling of wine and thyme, tickled my cheek. "His ways are not our ways, daughter. They are higher. We can't understand, but we can obey."

My chin shivered, making answering him difficult. "Yes, Father."

My father's reputation would soon lie in ruins. And it was all my fault. No man would ever marry me. I was sullied. I tried to imagine sharing this house with Father and Anna and the young ones, carrying my own child bound to my chest. Anna would dislike me even more. It would be worse than a death sentence.

And so I sobbed late into the night. Did I even weep this much when my mother died? My pillow muffled the anguished sounds, so my siblings slept undisturbed around me.

I spilled so many tears that night I doubted the straw inside the linen cover would ever be dry again.

HILL COUNTRY

MY THIRTEENTH YEAR

*T*rudging up the switchbacks behind a donkey cart lost appeal by the end of a single hour. Forget spending three days enduring a similar view. Father's merchant friend sang or spoke softly to the animals, two mules with bulky packs and the donkey pulling the small, rickety cart. He might have been alone for all the attention he paid me. Perhaps he didn't mean to slight me. After all, most of his time on the road was solitary.

Apparently, the fee Father paid the man to escort me to the remote village didn't include conversation. The void left plenty of time for unwelcome thoughts to invade my mind. The meditations swarmed like flies on a pile of goat dung.

One thought kept repeating: everyone would think the worst of me. People talked about the Messiah coming, born to a virgin of the tribe of Judah. No one understood how it could happen. None of them would believe the goat-herding daughter of Heli—namely me—would be the vessel Jehovah used.

If I hadn't spoken to the heavenly messenger, I wouldn't believe it. I pictured my best friend, Sarai, telling me she was pregnant by the Holy Ghost. (Isn't that what the angel had told me?) I would want to believe her. Why would she lie? Yet, I knew it would sound like boasting. If I couldn't imagine believing my own best friend, how could I expect anyone to accept the story from my mouth?

Father believed me. For now, that would be enough.

The meeting with Joseph would wait until I returned from my visit in the hill country. I had not seen Elisabeth, my cousin, since after my mother's death. Had it really been so long? I counted my brother Jesse's birthdays and decided it had been seven years.

Elisabeth's kindness helped our family through a difficult time. After Mother was gone, she stayed with us for two months. She's the one who found an acceptable wet nurse for my brother Jesse and showed me, just a young girl then, how to take care of a family. Yes, a girl of six years was expected to bear the responsibility for two children and a farm house.

Even then, she had been an old woman, my grandmother's age. Yet, the heavenly messenger said she would soon bear a son. How could one such as she bear fruit in her womb?

It was a miracle of God, the messenger had said. How would she feel? Would I be able to help her? Would she believe me if I told her about the messenger? Somehow, I knew I would find comfort in her bosom.

And so I climbed on, breathing dust through the thick

wool of my shawl, which I pressed tightly over my mouth and nose. I endured the rocks cutting into the soles of my sandals. When my ankle twisted in a rut, I pushed the pain to the back of my mind. I focused on what lay at the end of my journey: a mother's warm embrace offered by Elisabeth.

Perhaps, I would have solace of my own to offer her.

Or maybe I wouldn't speak about my problems, as Father had instructed. It would be months before my body revealed the secret. Joseph should be the first to learn of it. I wondered if he would think I betrayed my vows while on this excursion. Did it matter?

I sopped up a tear with a corner of my shawl—one I hoped wasn't dusty. My heart ached at the thought of wounding Joseph.

When Joseph set me aside, no other man would want me, not even for a second or third wife. My fatherless child would chain me to spinsterhood. Father's reputation would suffer, making it more difficult for him to make a match for my sister Mary, who was little more than a year younger than me. I would be shunned by the women in town. Being my friend would be tantamount to social annihilation. Who would risk it?

After a third full day of travel, we neared the end of the journey. Night fell before we reached the small dwelling Elisabeth shared with her priestly husband, Zacharias. Flickering candlelight offered welcome from behind the wooden shutters.Exhaustion made my legs feel like boulders, and the small pack of belongings on my back pressed down like a sleeping goat. Wrestling with my worries hadn't helped.

I knocked on the wooden door. The mules snorted and stomped behind me. The merchant delivered me to my relatives. His part was done.

With the light behind her, I couldn't distinguish the features of the woman who opened the door. Her voluminous robe covered her midsection but not the fact that she was expecting. A mound pressed against the front of her dark blue caftan. Her hair, pulled securely into a roll at the base of her neck, was mostly white with only a few dark threads running across the top.

"It's late, child." She tugged me into the house. "Zacharias has already retired for the night."

I wanted to apologize, but she shushed me and hustled me toward the table where the dripping candle offered light to the room. Her fingers tugged my pack from my back, but I pulled it to my chest, unwilling to let her bear it in her condition.

I greeted her. "You look well, cousin."

The shake of her head stopped. Her dark eyes widened, and the front of her robe bounced. The child moved! I wanted to reach out and touch the squirming mound but restrained myself. Anna had despised it when anyone touched her stomach when she was expecting.

"Blessed art thou among women," [1][xvi]Elisabeth cried, dark eyes glowing with a strange sheen, words echoing with authority.

"And blessed is the fruit of thy womb." Elisabeth threw her arms wide, as if to embrace me. "And whence is this to me that the mother of my Lord should come to me?"[2][xvii]

I allowed her to hug me, amazed when her child kicked through her skin and clothes and into my side. Tears leapt into my eyes. I had been more emotional in the past four days than I had been since my mother's death. If Father's wife's pregnancies were any indication, it would only get worse as my condition progressed.

Even as I reveled in her warmth, I wondered how Elisabeth knew I was expecting the Messiah.

"Your greeting?" I tried to ask about it.

"Lo, as soon as the voice of thy salutation sounded in mine ears, the babe leaped in my womb for joy."[3xviii]

Her interruption didn't stop the babe's churning. Did it hurt to have something rolling inside her like that?

I stepped back. My shawl dropped to my shoulders. Elisabeth's spotted and wrinkled hands cupped my face. Her calloused fingers smoothed away the moisture worrying my cheeks.

"Blessed is she that believed, for there shall be a performance of those things which were told her from The Lord."[4xix]

A strange peace engulfed me, and words poured from my mouth. For the first time, praise blotted out the fear.

The Lord had chosen me. It would not be easy, and most people would criticize and mock me. None of those things mattered. The Messiah was coming. God had promised this blessing to our Father Abraham, and now his ancient promise was being fulfilled. One so mighty could surely sustain me through the tumult ahead.

Both of us were crying when I finished my pouring out the praise to our Lord. Not tears of sorrow—tears of joy and shared comprehension. God had a special purpose for the sons we carried. Bearing the scorn of neighbors seemed a small price to pay in exchange.

As I write these words, once again I must say, "Blessed be Yahweh, whose words are as sure as the sunrise."

3

NAZARETH - SHEVAT

MY THIRTEENTH YEAR

*W*hat a welcome home! I bolted outside and heaved into the waste bucket until I thought my stomach might rend in half. I vomited until all that came out was a thick green slime. It burned my throat as it erupted from my mouth.

It was beginning. I pressed my sleeping shift against my stomach. Elisabeth warned me to expect as much as a month of nausea, usually just in the mornings. She kept flat bread beside her sleeping couch, claiming it helped to have something in the stomach before trying to stand up in the mornings.

I didn't know if I would be able to convince Anna to let me leave food beside my bed. Even if she allowed it, my brothers might eat it before I did. Those three were always hungry.

I clutched my stomach and returned inside. Tonight, Father and I would meet with Joseph. He had built a new house in town beside his shop. Father told me Joseph had been traveling for much of the time I was visiting my cousins. Did he wonder why I left so suddenly without a word to anyone?

Father told me nothing of his plan to approach the subject of my sudden pregnancy. Neither of us expected Joseph to uphold his end of the espousal agreement, not that we spoke our doubts aloud. An honorable man like Joseph bar Jacob would find infidelity an unacceptable breach of contract. How could I defend my virtue when my body told a different story?

Darkness fell early. Father and I walked to the village and down a small street far from the town's center to a sturdy brick building. Joseph's house (would it ever be mine?), a simple two room box, had sturdy wooden furnishings. Two pillows were nestled together near the hearth. Father lowered himself onto one of them. I stared toward the ground and nearly missed Joseph's gesture for me to sit on the other pillow.

Father shook his head.

"Thank you," I said, raising my eyes as far as Joseph's beard, "I will share with Abba."

Joseph nodded. "Would you care for wine, Father Heli?"

"Not at the moment."

I squatted beside Father on the edge of the pillow, my back resting against his side. Joseph folded his legs beneath him and nodded to Father respectfully.

In the light of the candles flickering on the nearby table, I studied this man, my betrothed. Flecks of gray dotted his dark brown beard, which he kept closely trimmed to his face. His skin was sun-darkened and weathered.

Pale brown eyes stared at Father. The planes of his face were broad and masculine, accentuated by his neatly trimmed hair, which hung to the collar of his robe in the back but was brushed away from his face in the front. It wasn't a traditional haircut, but it made sense for a man who bent over wood and stone, working with tools all day.

The two exchanged greetings and small talk, while I watched Joseph from beneath my lashes. I pulled my shawl further forward to camouflage the inappropriate staring.

"This is more than a social visit," Father said.

Joseph nodded. "Of course."

I felt Father glance toward me. I clenched my skirts with suddenly cold hands. Tightness in my chest made breathing difficult.

"Something unexpected has mired our betrothal agreement," Father said. "In days to come, you will surely hear many unflattering accounts of loose behavior and speculations against my Mary's character. An honorable man should never learn things in such a manner."

Joseph tilted his head toward Father, but his eyes swept in my direction. Heat clawed up my neck and burned my cheeks.

"Just over three months ago, Jehovah's messenger visited Mary."

A whisper of wind could have knocked me backward at that moment. Father said we would keep the truth from everyone, and yet he was telling Joseph. I glanced toward my future husband, wondering how he would react to the unbelievable account.

His face didn't change while Father repeated the angel's declaration. A calloused brown hand smoothed his beard. He cupped his chin in one hand, a finger straying to cover his strong mouth.

Father's direct approach shouldn't have surprised me. Of course he would tell Joseph. How else would he explain my condition?

"Mary is with child," Father said. "Although she has done nothing to violate the marriage contract, the law gives you the right to divorce her."

Joseph's brown eyes filled with emotion. I guessed it was disbelief. My experience spotting Anna's disapproval and condemnation made it easy to rule out those emotions. He rested his gaze on me, and I tried to shrink into my robe, wishing for a larger shawl to hide my embarrassment.

If he spoke to me, what would I say? The whole thing sounded absurd when Father admitted it aloud.

"You realize how incredible this sounds?" Joseph drew each of his words out, as if carefully selecting them.

"Yes. Precisely why no one outside this room knows about it."

Not exactly true. I had wanted to tell Father about Elisabeth's prophecy, but the trip had worn me beyond fatigue. Too tired to eat dinner, I had gone directly to bed when I arrived the previous day.

"You are claiming she is carrying the Messiah," Joseph said.

"I claim nothing. I am simply repeating what happened."

If what Elisabeth said was true, I would see this son rise to a position of importance. If Jehovah knew how scared the thought of being set aside by Joseph and shaming my father made me, would he still choose me? After all, I was no one. And now, his special child would be worse than an outcast and raised by a woman considered to have a loose reputation.

"I'm expected to believe my wife is pregnant but didn't have marital relations with another man?"

Father's silence made my stomach clench. Bile burned the back of my throat. I gritted my teeth, keeping the churning acid from making an escape. If I vomited here, I would die.

"I expect you to accept my word, one honorable man to another."

Silence filled the space around us. It was so complete I could hear the fire hissing against the lard on the candle nearest to me. Father expected too much.

"A large request, Heli," Joseph said. His face unreadable, voice unchanging; the man's emotions mystified me. Did he think Father lied to him?

No arguing—it was an amazing tale. So why should he believe it? Especially with his honor at stake.

By some miracle of faith, if he agreed to marry me, people would say we had prematurely consummated the wedding contract. If he broke our agreement, folks would believe I had stepped out during the engagement.

"I will respect whatever decision you make." Father never once dropped his gaze from Joseph's.

Silence dripped. Time dragged. My feet itched to run

away while my stomach tumbled, threatening to disgorge the lentils and bread I'd eaten for supper.

"I will consider your words and weigh my options," Joseph said.

He rose smoothly, bowing his head in reverence to my father. I scrambled to my feet, steadying Father as he stood. Creaks and groans sounded from his joints, reminding me that he was no longer a young man. How much had my predicament aged him?

Tears burned my eyes, blinding me from seeing the final exchange of glances between the men. I dared not spare a single look toward Joseph. Let his dismissal of me arrive in a writ on the morrow. It would be easier than hearing him denounce my father's honor in person.

That night, again, a flood of tears soaked my pillow. Is it true Jehovah keeps them all in a bottle? He will have to wring my pillow to capture the innumerable drops shed since his pronouncement.

4

NAZARETH - ADAR

MY THIRTEENTH YEAR

*T*hree days later, Joseph came to our farm shortly after sunrise.

I returned from milking the goats to see Joseph and my father in front of the house. Their heads were close together. No need to dwell on how my feet dragged, as if carrying a goat on every toe. As I drew closer, I studied the pot of milk I carried with great interest.

"Here she is." Father stepped toward me.

I stole a quick glance at Joseph. His gentle eyes watched me, but I could discover nothing from the stern set of his mouth and expressionless face.

"Joseph has news," Father said, sliding his arm across my back.

The heat from beneath his arm pressed against my shoulder. Father had been nervous. Did that bode well for my engagement? Or was it evidence I would hear more ill tidings?

Father cleared his throat, obviously waiting for Joseph to speak. When the silence stretched, it became too much for Father.

"Joseph has decided to honor the betrothal. He wishes to take you into his house immediately."

My gaze flew to Joseph's face. He studied me. Were his eyes softer than before? Or did I imagine the understanding behind them?

"Considering the circumstance, we'll forgo the wedding feast. Rabbi Natan will witness the vows, along with your mother and me."

"When?" My voice reminded me of a bird's squawk.

"Tonight."

Tonight? I would be married tonight?

My stomach lurched and churned. The dry flatbread I'd eaten before rising this morning threatened to return.

I sucked air through slightly parted lips, hoping to dispel the burn of acid at the back of my throat. Losing the contents of my stomach in front of my future husband would be the crowning moment of shame.

"I will come one hour before sundown," Joseph said.

More words were exchanged but I didn't hear. My ears rang with hissing and clanging. I suppressed the increasing need to vomit.

"This is wonderful news," Father said.

So wonderful I threw up beside the house when he moved off toward the fields. I wondered why Joseph changed his mind. We had been certain he would annul the agreement.

Thank you, Yahweh, for softening his heart toward me. Will I ever know how you accomplished such a miracle?

IT TOOK me a week to acclimate myself to life as Joseph's wife. Wife in every way except one. There had been no cloth on the wedding bed. In truth, there had been no wedding night exchange.

After our small ceremony, Joseph ushered me into the tiny sleeping area. The cubicle was curtained off from the living area with a hanging animal hide. He bid me good night and left me alone—in his bed.

The wooden frame covered with tightly bundled straw and rough linen bedding has been solely mine every night. I rose early one morning and saw Joseph sprawled atop the cushions Father and I sat on when we first visited the house. His lower legs hung over the edge. It looked uncomfortable.

When I suggested he take the bed, he made a stubborn face.

"You are with child," he said. Apparently, that was enough of an argument because he refused to discuss it further.

Today, I prepared a stew with a leg of goat Father had delivered earlier. We used the flat rounds of bread I had made to scoop the thick broth, vegetables, and meat into our mouths.

"I wondered if you would tell me something." My voice wavered slightly on the last word.

Joseph glanced up from his bowl, a loaded piece of bread

suspended midair. He nodded. Head and hand gestures comprised half of his vocabulary. So different from Father. But I was learning to understand him.

"Why did you change your mind about marrying me?"

He swallowed his food and settled his hands on either side of his nearly empty bowl. I noticed his blunt fingertips were stained. He worked hard but never spoke of it.

"What makes you think I changed my mind?"

I know my face showed my surprise. I had learned to hide much emotion from Anna, but I had never played those games with a man before. I refused to do it with my husband. Shouldn't husband and wife share everything?

"I shamed you and Father." I couldn't make eye contact. The succulent stew in my bowl looked unappetizing. "You had every right to dissolve the contract."

Joseph ate until his bowl was empty. I stood, turning toward the fireplace to refill it. His warm calloused hand on my wrist halted me.

"Jehovah sent a messenger to me, as well."

As well? He believed my story! My knees felt weak, and I stumbled back against the cushion, sitting down hard enough to force the air from my lungs.

"In a dream, the messenger told me to not fear taking you as my wife. He said the child had been conceived of the Holy Ghost."[1xx]

My mouth gaped. I snapped it shut, jarring my teeth together. God had spoken to Joseph too, and now he believed.

"What else did he say?"

Joseph stood and served himself another bowl of stew. I

watched his broad back as he bent over the fire. This was the longest conversation we had shared since our wedding.

"We will name our son Jesus."[2][xxi]

Jesus. Savior. Yes, that was the correct name. My fingers pressed against my mostly flat stomach. When I bathed, I noticed a slight rounding beneath my belly button. No one else would notice for a few more months.

"So you believe me about the baby?"

Joseph nodded, his attention focused on scooping more stew into his mouth. Studying the top of his head told me nothing.

When he finished eating, he thanked me for the satisfying meal. I sat like a sculpture. His eyebrows pressed together.

"Are you feeling alright?"

Worry. He sounded like Father when I fell in the cave and slashed my knee open on the rocks.

"I don't understand."

His eyes brushed over my face and frame. Hands clenching the bowl, he stared at me and nodded. It was his way of encouraging me to ask him for clarification.

"Why don't you . . ."

Heat flooded into my cheeks. Nothing in my life prepared me to ask a man about something so personal, even if the man was my husband.

"We don't . . ."

My mouth would not form the words. I decided to try sign language. I gestured toward the skin hanging in the doorway separating the sleeping chamber.

Understanding dawned on his features. His lips pressed

together. He wasn't sure how to address the subject, either. His obvious discomfort eased the tension in my shoulders.

"The messenger said I was not to know you as my wife until after the child is born."

A maelstrom of emotions pelted my stomach and mind. Relief that he didn't find me unattractive. Warmth for his willing obedience. Worry that the waiting would cause problems for us. Disappointment. It stopped the other thoughts. I was sad that I would not become his wife for nearly six more months.

"I'm sorry if that caused you worry," he said. "I figured you might be relieved not to have those attentions."

Now my eyes studied his face. He glanced down at the table top and rubbed his hand over a dark spot in the wood. It amazed me to realize he felt insecure about our marital relations, too.

I leaned forward and covered his hand with mine. Scrapes marred several of his fingers. A long scratch, scabbed over, ran across the back of his hand parallel to his wrist. Warmth flooded me where our skin touched.

One day we would be husband and wife completely. Something in my future would be normal.

5

CENSUS - AV

MY FOURTEENTH YEAR

*T*he arrival of the news altered my routine.

Sweat rolled across my forehead and onto my nose, threatening to drop into the jar I filled with water. Women left a wide gap on either side of me. I was little more than a social leper. Those closest to me turned their backs, confirming the intentional shunning.

Not that it mattered. Four months ago, I began to show signs of pregnancy but not enough to raise suspicion. Once my stomach pressed against the front of my robe, the mathematical calculations began. My friend, Sarai, congratulated me at this very spot—beside the city well. I didn't see her again for a week and when I greeted her, she quickly turned away.

"Heli taught her better."

"Such a shame to have a dishonorable daughter. I must keep my girls away or she'll surely corrupt them."

The gossip cut like a knife. It shamed me that Father's

character was being questioned because of me. Once the women wagged their tongues, some men withdrew orders from Joseph. That was even worse than the words.

I apologized to him several times.

"Enough."

Without raising his voice, he made it clear the subject was closed. Father's voice had the same stern quality.

"Jehovah has chosen you. What other people say means nothing."

"But your business—"

"Will recover eventually. People forget once the next rumor comes along."

Unfortunately, Nazareth was too small for many exciting tidbits to usurp my place as the center of negative attention. And so, I spoke to no one except when I visited my sister at the farm. It was a lonely time, and I often wished for my little herd of goats.

I returned to town with the heavy pot centered on my head.

Dust swirled as a rider drew up to the synagogue. I coughed and studied the Roman soldier. He unrolled a paper and nailed it beside the door. It was two days until the Sabbath, when all the men would meet to read from the Torah.

I dropped the heavy jar to my hip, moving to stand behind the other women who stopped their tasks to gawk at the soldier.

"Must be an important announcement."

"Why doesn't he read it out?"

"Romans are above consorting with Jews."

The old woman spat on the ground after making this statement. The spittle landed inches from my dusty toes. Not an accident, for certain. I paid her no mind.

Conversation lulled when the hammering ceased. A woman standing beside the millstone sent her oldest son to read the document. The rabbi and a few scribes had already emerged from within the synagogue to squint at the sign. The edges curled toward the center until one of the men pressed a hand over one corner.

Speculation swirled around me. Everyone agreed it was some sort of edict. Grim faces abounded. We knew, whatever the decree, it wouldn't have a positive impact on our community.

"A search for criminals."

"Don't want any of that type here."

"They would stand out in an instant. Folks don't come to Nazareth of Galilee to visit."

Laughter, both tittering and harsh, greeted this final claim.

I sighed and rested my pot and hip against the now idle millstone. The ragged donkey hung its head, paying no attention to the stir across the street.

The boy returned to his mother, panting, eyes flashing with excitement. Maybe it wasn't bad news after all.

I wanted to press closer, but experience had taught me that was the surest way to draw open rebuke. People would spread the news soon enough.

"Census?"

"Caesar decrees that every man must return to the city of his birth."

"When will this be?"

"Who will harvest our crops while we're gone?"

"Caesar cares nothing for our crops, only for his tax money."

"More taxes?"

"Why else would he need to take a census?"

The swirl of words dizzied me. I pressed my hands into the small of my back, arching to relieve the ache bending over the well had caused. The circular movement of my fingers pushed the knots around but didn't stop the discomfort.

Joseph's father, Jacob, had been born in Bethlehem. My grandfather, Matthat, had also been born there, but since my father was born in Nazareth, he wouldn't travel so far. It was seventy miles from Nazareth to Bethlehem.

I heaved the water pot back onto my head and hurried home to share the news with my husband.

~

Four weeks later - Elul

More than two dozen travelers left Nazareth together, Joseph's cousin among them. On the second day, those who traveled faster left us behind. Only ten remained, mostly old men and women and another expectant mother, barely showing.

By the third full day of travel, my throat felt like the cloth Joseph used to smooth his wooden furniture. Dust coated my exposed skin, making me itch, which resulted in grit beneath my fingernails to match what was between my teeth.

My feet throbbed for the first two days. The rawness on my soles screamed when I collapsed onto our rolled blanket.

How can I travel this way for two more days? When I reached for the stores of bread and jerky at the center of my rolled possessions, my back spasmed. I froze midmotion. My breath stalled in my lungs, and the added pressure of the trapped air increased the tearing pain.

"What's wrong?"

Joseph's concern loosed the tears that gathered when the agony struck. I tried to wipe the moisture away with the sleeve of my robe before he saw it. Didn't he have enough worries? A wife in need of coddling would certainly not be an asset at the moment.

"My back," I gasped. Another bolt of pain flashed across the muscles at the base of my spine.

Joseph knelt on the ground, his own pack still across his shoulders, and placed a gentle hand on my lower back. Sweat glued the fabric to my skin but the sudden heat from his hand soothed the knots. With slow strokes, his hand slid across my tight muscles. I relaxed, and air filled my lungs, chasing away the lightheadedness.

"It's too early," he whispered against my ear.

I nodded. It should be another two weeks before the baby comes. Not that today would be dangerously early, but delivering a child in the midst of strangers without a midwife would be less than ideal. And certainly not fitting for the special child I carried.

Joseph unrolled my blanket and handed me water, bread, and jerky. After laying his own blanket beside mine, he removed my shoes. Exposure to the air felt good on the sores caused by the continual rubbing of leather against my ankles and instep. But when he dabbed at the abrasions, I sucked air. He applied a salve, apologizing that he didn't have water to clean the wounds first.

I tried to keep my eyes open and watch Joseph interacting with the others. Once the bread and meat staved off my hunger and the water doused my thirst, my eyes could no longer refuse my body the rest it craved.

MY FEET THANKED Joseph for procuring me a seat atop the smelly gray donkey. The rattling cart the beast pulled drowned the stream of complaints from its owner. Why did he consent to let me ride if he was just going to moan about carrying the extra load?

I glanced at Joseph, striding beside the donkey, near enough to steady me over rough patches in the road. One hand rested on his wooden staff, and the other hovered always close to my knees. A bundle of wood was strapped beneath his rolled blanket. He had exchanged his comfort for my own. How could he bear all the extra weight?

My backside grew numb after the first hour. My legs refused to hold me when we stopped for a midday rest at a small oasis at the border of Judaea. Joseph slid his arms around my waist and held me against his chest, the child crushed between us. Several kicks to the front of my abdomen made known the babe's discomfort in the situation. Joseph's eyes widened, and he stared down at my bulging belly.

"So strong," he said, setting me away from him but keeping his hands firmly on my waist.

Blood rushing through my backside and legs caused a grimace to replace the smile on my face. Now my rear end throbbed rather than my feet. Only time would determine whether that was a positive exchange.

Another nudge inside me brought my hands to my abdomen. I gently massaged circles near the base of my ribs where the movement originated, smiling as the babe pushed against my fingers.

I stood for the entire break, sipping water and chewing on the travel rations. The shade overhead relieved the beginnings of a headache from the constant glare of the sun.

Would this journey ever end?

6

BETHLEHEM - ELUL

MY FOURTEENTH YEAR

The sun's last rays kissed the walls of Bethlehem as our group straggled within view of the city. Rather than heading toward the gates, Joseph followed a well-worn path to the east. His uncle lived outside the walls, near the shepherds. He spun cloth from the sheep's wool and grew a supply of linen on a small plot of ground. Most farmland stretched further to the west, away from the meandering sheep. Or maybe away from the shepherds, who weren't considered the cleanest of people.

We parted from the other travelers, including the grumbling man and his donkey. My feet protested against walking. I rubbed my lower back, stretching my shoulders to relieve the pressure. It would be good to sleep on a mattress again. The hard ground hadn't done any favors for my already stressed muscles.

Joseph lessened his stride so I could remain beside him.

Bleating and the familiar odors of sweat and dung eased my anxiety. These were smells and sounds of home. A group of keepers milled around the low walls of a sheepfold. Three stood in the doorway.

One goat rubbed its head against a shepherd's leg. A twinge of sadness poked my heart. I missed my goats. My sister Mary cared for them, but she had given up the cheese-making. My mouth watered at the idea of spreading the soft, fresh goat cheese on bread. Perhaps Joseph's uncle would invite us to join his table for dinner. Anything other than stringy dried meat sounded appealing.

The pathway widened into a well-traveled track with deeper ruts. I stumbled on a rock, too busy gazing at the shorn fields to watch my step; the advancing twilight didn't help matters. With a strong hand on my upper arm, Joseph steadied me. Our pace slowed even more. I yearned to arrive at his uncle's house, but my legs rebelled against moving any faster.

The smoky odor of cooking meat made my stomach rumble. I pressed my fingers over it and earned a kick from the babe. Out of the shadows, two buildings emerged beside the road.

From the larger of the structures, candlelight flickered invitingly. It was a flat-topped adobe building, common in Nazareth for merchants and shop owners. It was strange to see one outside the city walls.

I stood behind Joseph when he knocked on the door. It seemed a long while before the man appeared in the doorway. He had more gray hair than Joseph, but otherwise didn't seem much older.

"Joseph," the man said. His eyes slid toward me and he stepped outside, joining us in front of the house. "Your cousins arrived yesterday."

"Travel was difficult," Joseph said.

Uncle Biram nodded. "I have no room left in the house."

He seemed embarrassed to admit this, looking toward the ground rather than directly at Joseph.

"The roof would be fine. Something for Mary to sleep on is all we really need."

His uncle's gaze rested on me, sliding down to where my hand rested on my distended abdomen. His eyebrows drew together. Would there be no escaping the judgmental scowls? We were miles from home and the untimeliness of my motherhood still garnered speculation.

"The roof is where we put Nadab and his family. They arrived two days ago."

Joseph nodded. Were we being turned away by his family? Trembling started in my lower legs. I leaned into Joseph's broad back. Behind his uncle, the door to the house opened and a woman emerged, holding a candle in a shallow pottery dish.

"Biram? Oh, it's Joseph. Hello."

"Aunt Leah." Joseph nodded his head in respect.

"I was just telling them about our full house," Biram said.

"This crazy census." Aunt Leah shook her head, corners of her generous mouth turning down.

"I can find other accommodations tomorrow. If you could at least spare some floor space for one night—"

I could see Uncle Biram opening his mouth to deny this

plea. Shame and anger clashed in my gut, making the empty organ churn. The baby kicked against my ribs.

"The barn," the woman said. "We've room in there for you."

I turned to gaze at the other building, stone and wood, shabbier than the adobe structure. It would be out of the wind and cooling night air. Perhaps I would find clean straw to mound into a pallet. It would be an improvement over sleeping beside the road. My back cramped at the thought of another night on the sun-hardened earth.

"Thank you."

"I'll bring some food out," she said. "I see you have blankets."

"Sorry I couldn't offer you something more." Biram sounded apologetic, and his gaze didn't stray toward me this time.

"Times are hard for everyone, Uncle," Joseph said.

He turned to me, face in shadow. His fingers closed around my elbow. We moved toward the barn. Behind us, the door to the house closed.

"It's because of me."

Joseph draped his arm over my shoulder, pulling me against his side. My head nearly fit there.

"My cousins came to register. You heard them."

"The way he looked at me . . ."

"I'm sorry." His lips pressed against the top of my head, reminding me of something my father did when I was a much younger girl. When would we have a normal husband and wife relationship? Maybe never. Nothing was normal for me now. It never would be.

I swallowed away the tears. The dark doorway into the barn loomed before us. Stepping inside, the familiar scents of animals and manure embraced me. Tension drained from my shoulders.

I would be more comfortable here than in a house full of condemning relatives.

7

THE BABE - ELUL

MY FOURTEENTH YEAR

Four days after our arrival, I awoke to a band of tightness across my pelvic area. Not pain exactly, more like my muscles were flexing, except I hadn't told them to do anything. The sensation passed in moments. Floating on the scent of straw and livestock, I relaxed against my blanket, enjoying Joseph's warmth pressing against my back.

Tendrils of sleep fogged the edges of my thoughts. My abdomen tightened again, and my eyes popped open. I slid my hand to my midsection, feeling the skin straining. Today was the day.

I rubbed my hand over the mound covering my son. Soon I would meet him. I closed my eyes, knowing I needed to rest. No sense disturbing Joseph. In most cases, childbirth required the better part of a day.

Hours later, Joseph's cousin's wife, Delia, wiped my brow with a warm wet cloth. She shushed and hummed as if comforting a sick child. I closed my eyes, focusing on the gentle snuffling of the goats in the pen behind us.

"The head is crowning," Aunt Leah said. "The hardest pushes will be these next few."

Pain tore across my abdomen, and the urge to push against it overwhelmed any thought. I bore down, grunting. My fingernails dug into Delia's shoulders while her arms supported me, keeping me in the birthing squat. When the contraction passed, my legs quaked.

Aunt Leah helped Delia lower me against the rolled sheets piled atop a mound of hay. In the days since our arrival, the women had found burlap sacks for me to stuff with straw and cover with our blankets for a bed. All of that had been tugged out of the barn when the active labor began.

How long ago? It seemed like days but the shadows outside the door announced only midafternoon. The thought of calculating time slipped away as Delia dabbed perspiration from my forehead with the cloth. Sweat stung the corner of my left eye anyway.

I gasped as another contraction flared, wrapping my abdomen and lower back in a wreath of agony. They helped me up into the squat. I pressed against Delia with my fingers and the baby with my pelvic muscles.

"Breathe," Aunt Leah said.

All the air whooshed from my lungs when the pain rolled away. I panted slightly while

Aunt Leah studied my progress. "Three more like that," she said.

My whole body trembled like a leaf in a windstorm. How

could I push so hard three more times? I slapped away the cloth when Delia tried to pat my forehead again.

Grunting, pushing, and heaving. No work I had ever done in my life required the strain that birthing this child into the world did.

"One more," she said. She must have repeated those words ten times, until I was sure the contractions and pushing would never end.

The incredible pressure released after the next straining, groaning moment of agonizing labor. From beneath the raised umbrella of my skirt, Aunt Leah withdrew a wet, red mass of squirming flesh. She tilted him to the side, turning him over to remove the mucus from his mouth. His cry pierced the air, a single note of introduction.

The screaming mouth dominated his wrinkly face. Black hair covered the crown of his head. His clenched hands flailed in time with his crying.

I hardly noticed the next contraction or the feeling of pushing the placenta out of my body. When Delia leaned me against the pile of sweaty linens, I held my arms out. Months of feeling the change in my body, watching my stomach grow larger and larger, were at an end. Memories of being snubbed at the well or millstone faded into nothing.

A shadow passed in front of the doorway. Joseph. Of course he hadn't gone far. He had taken his mission of caring for me and the baby more seriously than anything else.

"A son," Aunt Leah said, placing the naked mass of red flesh across my chest.

My son. He opened his eyes and stared at me. I saw my own pale, sweaty features in the depths of those reflecting pools. I stroked his damp hair. My finger trailed down his cheek. He turned his mouth toward it, catching my knuckle between his lips. The suction startled me.

"Hungry," Delia said, helping me slide the top of my sweat-soaked shift aside and free my breast. "Some babies aren't interested for hours."

"Good sign," Aunt Leah grunted, rising to her feet clutching a mass of bloody straw in her hands. "Massage her stomach, Del."

All that mattered were those black eyes, alert and lucid, staring at me. My younger siblings had squirmed and squalled and slept right away.

When I touched my nipple to my son's cheek, he turned and immediately latched on. I gasped. I cupped his head in my other hand, watching as his eyes twitched and finally closed. Still, he suckled.

A well of maternal joy flooded my heart. My son snuggled to my breast. A sense of rightness welled. Now, my life was complete.

SHUFFLING outside the barn startled me awake. A strange white glow cast long shadows in front of the open doorway. I reached out, touching the edge of the manger beside my head.

Joseph stirred from his place on the opposite side of the manger. When he stood, the indistinct scuffles coalesced into the sound of approaching footsteps. A goat bleated from the other side of the doorway.

After helping me sit up, Joseph glanced toward the

manger. Even in the gloom, I saw his features soften. He loved my son. My heart expanded in my chest. Jehovah had blessed me with an honorable man. I breathed a soft prayer as Joseph turned toward the doorway, exiting to see what the commotion was about.

"An angel." A voice drifted in.

"Bright light."

"Look."

Joseph spoke too softly for me to make out his words. His deep voice tickled across my spine anyway. Who was he speaking with? It might be his uncle or cousins, but I doubted they would rouse themselves this early in the morning. Dawn was still several hours away, I guessed.

When he returned, Joseph knelt beside me. "There are shepherds here to see the baby."

I gaped at him. What an unattractive response to the unexpected visitors!

"Can they come in?"

I nodded, resting my hand on the soft fuzz peeking out from the layers of swaddling clothes. Since these strips were used for wrapping newborn lambs, they were readily available in the stable. I would make some proper clothes for my son, but for now, the strips binding his arms tightly to his body comforted him.

Four men and one goat followed Joseph into the cramped barn. The cozy atmosphere became oppressive.

"In a manger, as we were told," one of the shepherds said.

"Praise God," said another.

In the dim light, I could tell they were shepherds by their distinctive headdresses and the odor of sheep clinging to them. I smiled as the goat pushed its way between two of the men and stuck its nose in the manger.

"Get out of that," a younger voice said from the back.

The goat stopped, staring at me for a moment and then nuzzling the baby. His eyes snapped open. I prepared myself for his cries. None came.

Instead, he looked toward the group of men. Based on my time caring for my newborn siblings, I knew his sight was limited. Still, he seemed to stare at each one of them. A grizzled man in the front swiped at his cheeks.

"An angel startled us this evening."

"This morning, really."

"A couple hours ago. Told us the Christ had been born in Bethlehem."

Rather than fumbling over each other, their sentences seemed to complete the one before it. Awe and excitement laced the words. Something extraordinary had happened to them this night. I wanted to hear all about it.

"Tell the whole story," I said.

When I spoke, my son turned his head toward me.

"One angel lit up the sky," the old shepherd said.

"Scared me into a statue," another said.

"Told us not to fear. He had good tidings for all people."

"For unto you is born this day in the city of David a Savior, which is Christ the Lord."[1][xxii] This from the youngest shepherd, still behind the others. Could he even see the child?

"Told us a sign."

The old shepherd nodded. "Said we would find the babe wrapped in swaddling clothes, lying in a manger."[2][xxiii]

I covered my gasp of shock with one hand. I don't think any of them noticed, but I saw Joseph's gaze sweep across me.

"Then, a whole crowd of angels filled the sky."

"They chanted and praised God. Better than all the worship I've heard up in Jerusalem."

"Glory to God in the highest."

"On earth, peace, good will toward men."[3][xxiv] The young shepherd's voice crackled with enthusiasm.

"Messiah is come," the old shepherd said. This time I knew he wiped a tear from his face with the sleeve of his robe.

A strange aura of worship entered the room. In turn, each of the shepherds knelt before the manger. The babe turned his dark eyes toward the strangers, and I got the impression he saw each one.

The emotional elder shepherd knelt on the packed dirt floor after the others had finished. He reached out a spotted and wrinkled hand toward the baby's forehead. Anxiety flickered across my stomach. No mother wanted a stranger touching her child.

The way the baby stared at the old man made my tension subside. Rather than crying in the face of strangers, he seemed calm and accepting. I reminded myself that he was no ordinary child. It wouldn't be the last time I had to do that, either.

"The savior, Christ the Lord," the old shepherd whispered.

His gnarled fingers grazed the babe's hair before the meat of his hand rested on my son's forehead, standard form for a blessing. "Praise the God of Abraham, Isaac, and Jacob for fulfilling His promises. Great is the Lord and greatly to be praised."

Tears streaked down the old man's face. Yet, his eyes remained on the babe. He seemed unashamed of the emotions welling from deep within.

He turned his face toward me. "Bless you, mother of Messiah."

He stood, turning and exiting without another glance. At the door, the young shepherd watched the entire scene. His face, shadowed by the doorway, turned toward the babe once more before he followed the old man.

As much as I had never expected to bear my first son in a stable and give him a feed trough for a cradle, the visitation of the shepherds was stranger still. Jehovah didn't work through happenstance. These men, who provided the daily temple sacrifices, had received a heavenly visitation.

The babe mewled and let out a single cry. I leaned over and pulled him to my chest, adjusting the front of my robe so he could be fed. He quieted immediately. When I pressed him to my breast, he began to suckle. Tenderness drove my pondering away.

It wouldn't be the last time I wondered at these strange events.

JERUSALEM - TISHREI

MY FOURTEENTH YEAR

*J*esus was forty days old. My son snuggled against my chest and our hearts beat in unison. His breath warmed my neck, sending shivers into my stomach. Still so new, this precious life, but it was difficult to recall my world before he filled my arms.

Joseph pulled me into his side, out of the path of a man leading two donkeys laden with wood. I watched them lumber past, happy to be walking on my own two feet. It was only six miles to Jerusalem. Today I must offer a sacrifice for my purification. On the morrow, we will begin the long trek home to Nazareth. Will I soon be wishing I was riding one of those donkeys?

My stomach dropped at the thought of returning to Nazareth, so I contemplated my visit to the temple. I had only entered the temple on one other occasion. Even though it was a mere two years since I accompanied Father at Pesach, it may as well have been a lifetime. Important events, crammed like too many goats in a pen, filled those months, making them loom larger than all the months that came before them. Certainly I never expected to be bringing my firstborn to the temple at fourteen.

Over the milling crowd, I saw the narrow archway of the gate. Shepherds called it the sheep gate, but others called it the dung gate. In either case, the ripe smell rising from the crush of people heading in both directions wrinkled my nose. Forward motion ceased and started. Chickens squawked, sheep and goats baaed, the smell of manure and sweating flesh undergirded everything.

Thrusting my nose into the fine black hair atop Jesus' head, I inhaled the sweet scent of milk and infant. Joseph hugged me into his chest again as a cluster of smelly men jostled us. His beard scratched against my cheek. I glanced at him, noting his eyes scanned the baby's head before meeting mine. There was such a solemn set to those gentle brown orbs.

Outside the court of the Gentiles, several booths offered lambs, kids, bullocks, and birds for sale. Joseph approached one of the birders. I stood behind him listening as he bartered for the two turtledoves required for my sacrifice. The baby sighed against my chest. I glanced down. His wide, dark eyes stared at me.

"I hoped you would sleep through all this chaos," I whispered against his forehead.

Joseph turned, a small wooden cage with two birds swaying from his closed fist. I clenched his coat, so we weren't separated by the throng of worshipers. The tightly wrapped satchel containing much of our belongings bounced on his shoulder blades and into my temple. I shielded the baby's head with my hand, praying none of the people scraping against us had a sicknesses to spread to him. No wonder Anna never wanted to go anywhere when my brothers were infants-too much to worry about.

We had to wait in line to speak with a priest. Even in the courtyard overshadowed by the brass altar, the press of people made it impossible to relax and focus on the purpose of our visit. How did people worship in the midst of this human maelstrom? I tried to quiet my mind and pray, but the loud prayers of the priest nearby made it impossible to think.

Jesus squirmed against my breast. Surely he wasn't hungry. If he needed to be changed-I glanced in all directions-I didn't know where I could accomplish the task. Certainly nowhere clean or private.

A prayer sprung to my lips. "Yahweh, please keep the baby from needing to be fed or changed until we are finished with this."

It probably wasn't the holiest prayer of my life, but I hoped God would answer favorably anyway.

I reached to the knot tied in the middle of my lower back and loosened the fabric enough to move the restless baby into my arms. My gaze caught an older man across the courtyard staring at me. In this crush, he thought my baby was too loud?

"What is it?" Joseph leaned his face close to mine to be heard above the chorus of men who had begun praying.

"I'm not sure."

"Hungry?"

I shook my head. I had fed him less than two hours ago while we sipped water and ate the bread and meat supplied by the innkeeper.

"Here," a man said, stopping in front of me.

Both Joseph and I looked up at him. It was the man who had been staring!

He was much older than my father. A phylactery in the center of his forehead marked him as a zealot. Long gray hair lay in thick ringlets over his shoulders, and his beard hung to mid-chest—more marks of his piousness. His hands, smoother than Joseph's, stretched toward Jesus.

"Who are you?" Joseph angled his body to block the man.

"Simeon," the man said. "The Lord promised I would see His Christ today. I have come to bless him."

A bubble rose in my gullet. Why was this man making a scene? Too many people would notice.

"May I bless your son?" the man asked. His eyes grazed Joseph's face and settled on me. Was he truly asking my permission? How uncustomary.

My eyes flew to Joseph's face. He frowned, stepping aside so the man could reach toward us. His broad back coupled with Simeon's much narrower frame formed a sort of quiet triangle amid the storm of people.

I glanced at Jesus, noticing he had quieted. He faced the old man, eyes unblinking. I tucked the cloth around him so it wouldn't drag the ground when it fell from my waist and held him toward Simeon.

The man's features seemed to glow, as if lit from within.

His countenance reminded me vaguely of the messenger all those months ago.

"Lord, now lettest thou thy servant depart in peace, according to thy word."[1][xxv] The cadence of his words reminded me of Father's bedtime prayers. "For mine eyes have seen thy salvation." He stared at the babe. "Which thou has prepared before the face of all people: a light to lighten the Gentiles, and the glory of thy people Israel."[2][xxvi]

His words stunned me. As he spoke, the noise around us seemed to still. When he finished, he fixed tear-filled eyes on me and my breath caught in my throat.

One of his hands rested on my son's forehead, and the other cradled him. "Behold, this child is set for the fall and rising again of many in Israel: and for a sign which shall be spoken against."[3][xxvii]

Simeon raised his hand off Jesus' head and stepped closer to me. When he placed his palm on top of my head, heat radiated through the shawl covering my hair. Still, a chill slid down my spine. What was happening?

"Yea, a sword shall pierce through thy own soul also that the thoughts of many hearts may be revealed."[4][xxviii]

At his words, my heart leapt in my chest as it had when Elisabeth spoke her prophecy to me. I couldn't seem to get enough air. Joseph's arm rested against my shoulders and I leaned into him, wondering at my trembling legs.

An ancient woman several steps away raised her hands and shouted, "Praise the Lord God of Israel for His salvation."

Every hair on my body stood at attention. People stopped

talking and looked toward the old woman, whose hands remained uplifted.

After that, the prayer of the priest and the offering of the two doves seemed to blur into one continuous moment. My heart was full of dread at the man's words. Before the birds were pierced and burnt, I prayed for repentance and cleansing.

The old man's words, "A sword shall pierce through thy own soul," replayed in my mind. A knot tightened in my chest.

The old woman touched my shoulder as we shuffled away from the altar and toward the exit.

"Look for redemption," she said, her eyes full of tears and her lips trembling into a smile. "God's redemption has come to Jerusalem."

"Bless you, Mother," Joseph said to the old woman, pressing a copper coin into her hand.

Her eyes strayed to Jesus, swaddled in my arms, still gawking around as if absorbing the entire scene.

"Praise the Lord," she repeated, raising her hands to the sky. Jesus swung his gaze in her direction; his eyes met hers. The old woman began to weep.

Joseph pulled me close and shoved through the doors into the outer courtyard. In the open air, I should have been able to breathe again. Instead, the knot of dread camped beneath my ribs. Deep breaths were impossible. My vision blurred.

"A sword shall pierce through thy own soul," the devout man, Simeon, had said.

When? How could I continue with this prophecy of doom hanging over my head?

Jesus' fingers pinched the skin by my collar bone. I glanced down at him. His wide dark eyes stared into mine. Peace flooded through my chest.

Love swelled between us. I stroked his fine hair. As long as I had this precious boy, I could face that sword. I hugged him close, inhaling his milk-scented breath.

I would face anything to keep my son safe.

VISITORS - KISLEV

MY FIFTEENTH YEAR

Once Joseph and I returned to his home, life in Nazareth fell into a new but predictable pattern. For more than a year, my days revolved around caring for my baby boy and new husband—not leaving much time or energy for keeping a journal.

For many months, the shunning continued at the well and community gatherings. Finally, a few of the younger women, who had been friends with me in childhood, broke the barrier. Being included didn't matter as much now that I had my perfect son.

Jesus was perfect. (What mother says differently about her newborn child?) He was no more comely than any newborn, infant, or toddler, but his actions singled him out. Although he cried when he was hungry or needed changing, it was a gurgling sound, more like laughter than crying. Those screams that pierce eardrums or make the hair on your neck stand up? He never came close.

While other babies fussed about the heat in the summer, Jesus stared out with calm brown eyes. Sometimes his face would be ruddy and his shirt soaked with sweat when I returned home from the day's chores. Still, he didn't whimper or complain.

Being a mother was nothing new. After all, I had mothered Jesse when our mother died. I'd been the caretaker of my other siblings in the years since.

Being a wife was more difficult. Joseph remained something of a mystery. I learned that if he made no comment about a meal, he enjoyed it. Not that he ever spoke negatively about my cooking, but little things like "Is lamb usually so stringy?" let me know that he didn't prefer a dish. I peppered him with questions until he gave in and began to talk to me about his work. I hated the idea of being a contentious wife, but I hardly knew this man whose house I shared.

This day began as any other. Up before dawn to prepare breakfast for Joseph, feed Jesus, and milk the goat (I'm so thankful Father gave me the milk nanny when Mary became betrothed). Comforting thumps and sawing from the adjacent shop assured me that Joseph was hard at work.

Outside, I noticed an odd-shaped star beaming more brightly than the sun. Weren't stars for nighttime? This one had appeared in the sky two nights ago and seemed to grow larger with each passing hour.

After returning from the well, something that took more time now that the women shared news and discussed upcoming events with me, I brought my husband a fresh skin of water. He thanked me for the refreshment and informed me he would be delivering a table to one of the outlying farms. My father would lend him a yoke of oxen and a cart.

My husband left for his errand. I returned to the house, setting Jesus down to play while I worked on mending a tunic for Joseph. Humming a tune, I jumped when someone pounded on the door. I opened it to find a breathless Sarai, flushed from exertion.

"What is it?"

"A caravan of visitors is heading this way because of the strange light in the sky. I heard them say they followed the star from Jerusalem."

I stepped outside. The star shone brighter than before.

"Are they here to study it?"

Sarai shook her head, bouncing onto her toes. She hadn't been this excited since she showed me her wedding garments.

"They are coming here."

"Here?" I furrowed my brow, trying to wrap my mind around this news. "To this house?"

Her head bobbed with enough force to send her shawl onto her shoulders. She pointed up at the star. "Don't you see how it points to your house?"

I leaned inward, checking on Jesus, who sat happily on the floor stacking blocks Joseph had made from wood scraps.

I stepped away from the door and studied the sky. Sarai hadn't exaggerated. The star appeared to have a tail, and the long thin stream of light glinted onto the roof of our home.

What on earth? *Jehovah, what does it mean?*

Men's voices carried to my ears. The city elders strode onto our street. Joseph's shop sat on a minor side street near the southern boundaries of town. I didn't recall ever seeing the stuffy elders in our inconsequential neighborhood.

Four men wearing exotic robes and tightly bound turbans accompanied the elders. The strangers stared toward the heavens, rudely ignoring the elders' bowing and scraping. Two of the strangers had yellowish skin, and their eyes were slanted. I had seen Far Eastern traders only rarely in my mostly rural existence. Adorned in richly patterned red robes, their eyes dropped from the celestial anomaly to my humble stone house to me, stopping at my feet.

Of the other two strangers, one had the black skin of an Egyptian but wore strange clothing and his face was unpainted. The other's skin was a deeper brown than my own, and his flowing white garments were strangely untouched by the dirt swirling around his lower body. He stepped forward, ducking his head toward me in a reverential way.

My heart plummeted into my stomach. Who were these men? What did they want? Without my husband home, their presence at the house was improper. As if my reputation could suffer further damage.

"Is the child here?" His Aramaic was heavily accented, but I understood him.

"What child do you seek?"

"The one whose star we've followed. He who is born King of the Jews, a deliverer of nations and the Prince of Peace."

I must have looked like a fish while I opened and closed my mouth several times. How did they know about Jesus? Was it safe to admit who he was?

I glanced up to see the elders leaning closer, hungry for information. When the man saw me staring at the city fathers, he motioned to another man—a towering black-skinned servant—and the elders were herded like wayward sheep back up the street.

"Yes, my son is here."

Sarai glanced between me and the foreigners, saying nothing. Having her hovering near my elbow offered a strange sense of reality and comfort to the bizarre situation.

"Hallelujah!" the man shouted, startling me backward. He turned and communicated with the others in a foreign tongue. His arms gestured widely, and his tone sounded frantic. After his speech, he turned back to me and said, "We have traveled far and wish only to worship him."

And still, I had no idea how the star would have announced who Jesus was to these men. I clutched the corners of my headdress. Should I admit them? A compulsion to honor their request pushed at my chest.

"Welcome," I said, motioning for the men to enter through the wooden door, still ajar from my hasty exit.

Sarai's mouth gaped. I shooed her away, promising, with my eyes, to fill her in later. I followed the strangers, who clustered together, filling the small room and pointing to Jesus. I circled around them, afraid of the wide-eyed look on my son's face. My bare feet whispered across the dirt floor.

My bare feet! I wasn't even fully clothed. How could I be receiving these important men in such a state? I folded myself onto the floor behind Jesus, rubbing his downy brown hair.

My son dropped the block he held beside the small tower he'd constructed. Using my outstretched hand, he pulled himself to his feet. Though he'd been walking for a few months, he still preferred to climb up something in order to stand. Without hesitation, he stepped toward the cluster of strangers, who immediately ceased speaking.

I slid along the floor behind him, always within arm's reach, one hand propelling me forward and the other hiding my dirt-caked feet beneath my skirt.

As if in the throne room of Herod, the men knelt in front of my son, removing their turbans and bowing their heads. Jesus touched each of them in turn. His pudgy baby hand looked so small and pale against their black hair. The men murmured in their fast, clipped language when he stood beside them. Not once did they lift their faces from the floor. I had never seen such complete obeisance outside the temple walls.

These wealthy travelers worshiped Jesus. Somehow, they understood his prophesied destiny. The angel's words echoed in my mind, drowning the foreign voices, "The Lord God shall give unto him the throne of his father David: and he shall reign over the house of Jacob for ever."

A shadow passed in front of the door. One of the Easterners rose to his feet and spoke with the enormous black servant. Jesus lingered over the fourth man, his fingers fondling the dark brown hair.

"You honor me, Lord of Creation," the man said in Aramaic.

Jesus turned away, waddling past me and plopping down next to his stack of blocks. The audience with these men had ended for my sweet boy of fifteen months. He picked up the stray block and set it atop the tower, smiling when the tower didn't collapse.

"We brought gifts," the man said, standing now. He'd replaced the turban atop his head and it sat slightly askew.

I battled my desire to straighten it or smile at the lopsided display. I did neither. Instead, I nodded. It was customary for visitors to present gifts to royalty. My humble home, as clean, cozy, and peaceful as it might be, didn't seem appropriate for such an exchange.

One of the red-robed men stepped forward, bowing over his outstretched hands. In palms similar in color to mine, he held an ornate box engraved with foreign symbols. When I extended my hands, he placed the box in them. I stumbled forward at the weight. It was hardly an empty box.

I sidled over to the table, trying not to turn my back on our guests. I opened the lovely lid and gasped.

Inside, gold coins stamped with the Roman governor's likeness glinted in the sunlight slanting through the window. It was more gold than I had ever seen in one place. It must be enough for several years' wages for the wealthiest man in Nazareth.

I returned to the man and inclined my head as I had seen Joseph do when showing deference to someone. "What an amazing gift! You honor my son. Thank you."

The words felt inadequate in the face of such wealth. Even now, thinking back on it, I struggle to find any suitable expression for the gratitude I felt.

He bowed, backing away from me. The man who spoke Aramaic whispered something to him.

The other red-robed man bowed before me. In his extended hands he held a fired vessel. With intricate designs painted on the nearly white sides and a sealed lid stoppering the top of the bottle, I guessed it must contain some sort of perfume or oil. I nodded toward him as my fingers closed around the exotic container.

"A wonderful gift. Many thanks," I said. The man backed away, bowing repeatedly.

The dark-skinned man stepped forward, his stride billowing his deep purple cloak like the mane on a galloping horse. He knelt on one knee and balanced a small pot on his other. Again, the vessel looked like a perfume or oil container. The small opening at the top was corked with wax. A sparkling stone pressed into the wax would act as a handle. When he handed me the etched urn, I thanked him.

While placing the gorgeous pottery on the table, I stared at the stone. It was a deep purplish red. Had I ever seen anything like it in my life?

The first three men turned away and left me alone with the fourth man, who held a bag sewn from brightly colored cloth. An intricate pattern repeated over the shiny fabric. I took it, surprised by its weight.

"To you our gifts seem weighty," he said. I knew he referred to the costliness, but his choice of words when I struggled to heft the bag onto the table almost made me smile.

I nodded and opened my mouth to reply. He held up his hand in the universal signal for stop. I pinched my lips together.

"For generations, we have studied the sky, waiting for a sign that the deliverer had been born. It gives us joy to kneel in his presence and offer these tokens of our wonder, amazement, and adoration."

"Your tokens amaze and humble me," I said.

"Your son acted honorably, receiving us and offering his blessing. Some princelings have shown less courtesy to me."

"He's a good boy," I said. How woefully insufficient were my words!

As I write this, I wonder what this wealthy man from the East thinks of the King's mother. Even now, I don't know what words I should have said to show more gratitude.

"A Prince of Peace," the man said, bowing his head and exiting the house.

I followed him to the door. The others had already retreated. The lumbering servant fell into step behind the last visitor. I should have offered refreshment. What sort of welcome would they have received from a king's household?

I closed the door, deep in thought. Jesus stared up at me from the floor, blocks scattered around him and fingers buried in his mouth.

With one hand, I opened the magnificent bag. A glance inside stopped me in my tracks. More gold. Unmarked pebbles of varying sizes filled my hands. Another fortune.

Behind me, Jesus began to hum, the sound muffled by his hand. His empty stomach needed immediate attention.

I set the bag on the table beside the other three gifts. Priceless gifts. More than I ever imagined having.

I bent down and pulled Jesus into my arms, sliding him onto my left hip.

My lips brushed across his downy hair. The scent of

wood shavings emanated from his skin, so like Joseph's after a day in the shop.

"Let's get my little king some food," I whispered in his ear before planting a smacking kiss on his cheek. He grinned, turning toward the sound.

The unexpected gifts were more valuable than anything I had seen. Still, they were nothing in light of the ultimate gift filling my arms—and my heart.

EGYPT - KISLEV

MY FIFTEENTH YEAR

I would never have marveled so long over the visit from those strangers if I had realized what anxiety would follow. That very same night, my life was wrenched from its familiarity.

Joseph admired the gifts, carefully hiding the oils in a compartment he carved from the stone walls. They fit snugly, concealed by the stone in front of them. A simple tapestry draped over the spot hid everything.

After dinner, I lay Jesus in the wooden cradle Joseph had built for him. Sturdy and highly polished, it showcased my husband's skill. Crafted for all our children, he told me, sending a blush into my face. Jesus wasn't more than three months old at the time.

I hummed a lullaby and curled onto our mattress. Joseph extinguished the lamp and rolled into bed beside me before I fell completely asleep.

Then he was shaking me, his hand hot through my sleeping shift.

"Mary, wake up."

The urgency in his tone chased my weariness away. I bolted upright, staring through the gloom toward the baby's bed.

"An angel visited me. We must leave. The boy is in danger."

I covered a gasp.

"Pack everything. I'm going to the smithy. I think he had a donkey and cart for sale."

"Where are we going?"

"Egypt," he said, standing up and lighting an oil lamp, keeping the flame low. The shuttered windows should keep the light from seeping out, but his caution gave me pause.

Egypt? So far? It would take more than a week to travel there.

"Mary, we must hurry."

I stood, pulling the blanket toward me. "Who could ever hurt Jesus?"

"Herod wants to destroy him."

Tears pricked the corner of my eyes, and my mouth gaped. If the ruler of Judea and the surrounding provinces wanted to kill Jesus, how would we ever escape?

Joseph strode toward me and pulled me against his broad chest. Whether he read my mind or simply wanted to comfort me, I don't know. His strength fortified me.

"We will head to the coast," he said. "The Lord provided the gold we need to make this journey."

The gold. Of course. We wouldn't have to travel like the

peasants we were. Thanks to the strangers, we had enough money to flee into exile on a passenger ship. Was it thanks to them that Herod knew about Jesus' birth? Sarai told me they had come from the capital.

"Mary." Joseph stepped away, his calloused hands gripping my upper arms. "We need to go now."

I don't remember what I packed. By the time he returned, I had two bundles prepared for the journey. Jesus stirred when I lifted him from the cradle. I hummed in his ear, rubbing my cheek on his while Joseph arranged the bundle of bedding into a comfortable seat for me.

Strong hands spanned my waist when he lifted me into the small cart. It would be cramped, but I didn't complain. I remembered the long walk to Bethlehem and back.

Thank Jehovah I wouldn't have to walk all the way to Egypt.

~

NISAN - MY SIXTEENTH Year

Urgency chased us to Egypt, but the stay in the South seemed inconsequential. Joseph worked on a building project, earning enough money so we could keep the remaining gold hidden. Jesus grew. His steps became surer. He began to mimic words when I spoke to him. It was pleasurable to see Joseph's eyes brighten when Jesus called him father.

Four months after our arrival, Joseph arose early in the morning and began setting our possessions in order.

"The angel of the Lord says we can return home now," he told me when I questioned him. "Herod is dead."

A flood of relief made my arms weightless. As I prepared Jesus, I considered what this news meant. At last, we could return to Nazareth and resume our life. My lips moved in a prayer of gratitude as I bustled around our rented rooms, folding clothing items and sweeping the stone floor.

People speaking a multitude of foreign tongues pressed against us as we neared the port. Joseph secured passage on the next available vessel going to Joppa. The steward assured Joseph he could easily find a ship to take him farther north to Caesarea or Ptolemais.

The scent of unwashed bodies faded beneath the stench of fish. I clutched Jesus to my chest. His weight made my arms ache. He wasn't a baby any longer.

We stood on the dock, awaiting word from the porter that passengers were welcome to board. That's when I heard it.

"Got what he deserved, I say," a sailor said, his Aramaic accented but understandable.

Another man, who rolled barrels to the side of the ship and secured them to the rope that hauled them aboard, grunted.

"Lots of wickedness he committed," the first man said. "It's justice that he should die to sickness rather than in an honorable battle."

The second sailor tugged on a rope and guided the barrel past his head.

He grunted again. "He acted crazy. Killing all those babies a few months back."

My mind stumbled over this information. Herod killed

babies? While my family fled to safety, others paid the ultimate price? I never suspected Herod would harm any other child. Pain knifed through my chest. Was this the sword old Simeon had mentioned?

"Split his territory into three parts," the first man said, rolling another barrel forward from a dwindling stack on the dock behind him. "Didn't trust any one of his sons to rule it all."

The second sailor spit to the side. "Doubt things will be any better."

I choked back bile at the news of Herod's senseless murdering spree. What sort of evil compelled a man to murder innocent children? Tears glazed my vision. I pulled my shawl lower to cover my sorrow.

On the heels of my grief, another emotion swelled in my chest: satisfaction. It was the first time I was ever glad to know someone was dead.

But his death wouldn't bring back the innocent children. How many had he slain? I hugged Jesus closer, squeezing my eyes against the onslaught of tears.

Thank you, Yahweh, for keeping my son safe.

I could almost hear an echo, His voice whispering, "My son."

NAZARETH - IYAR

MY TWENTY-THIRD YEAR

*E*ven though Jesse added a room onto our childhood home, it felt cramped to me. Or it could have been the five children rushing in and out the doorway making me uncomfortable. My younger brothers may have been playful, but I didn't remember them acting that way. I didn't remember my childhood, which ended when I was six.

I shook thoughts of losing my mother away. My sister Mary squeezed my elbow.

"Anna wants to talk to you."

Memories of such talks from my youth crowded into my thoughts. I push them back. I'm a mother now. I can have compassion for my stepmother. The hard expression she wore when Father took my face in his hands and said, "You are exactly like her—body, soul and spirit," made sense to me now. Who could live in the shadow of an ever-present ghost? I couldn't imagine sharing my husband with another woman —even if she was nothing but a memory.

"Jesus, will you take the young ones outside," I said, motioning to my oldest. He sat against the wall beside the door, whittling a scrap of wood. Probably making another toy for his little sister.

"Yes, Mother," he said. "Do you want me to take Rachel?"

My youngest—finally a girl—was strapped to my chest, where she'd fallen asleep during the walk from the village. I shook my head. I didn't want to risk waking her, even if my lower back ached from the extra weight.

Jesus stood and grabbed the hands of his cousin James and his brother Simon. The three-year-olds chased each other on chubby legs until he corralled them with a touch.

"How about a game outside?" Jesus spoke quietly but with authority.

Judah, Mahlon, and my James barreled past the open doorway, cheering. They loved when Jesus wasn't working in Joseph's shop and could play with them. He certainly had more patience and energy than I ever did.

"How is Nomi?"

Mary shook her head. The girl had always been pale and sickly, but Jacob couldn't be persuaded to turn his interest elsewhere. Maybe older sisters worry too much, but I prayed this woman would be able to bear him a healthy son.

I pushed through the goatskin hanging over the doorway into the additional room. Inside, a bed, table, and stool filled the space. Woven rugs added color to the dirt floor. My step-mother sat on the stool, working wool with her birdlike hands.

I should have kissed her cheeks, a proper greeting for a mother, but we have never been close. I nodded to her instead and sat on the ground near her feet, cradling Rachel's warm body against my chest. *Lord, let her sleep on. Don't let my movements disturb her.*

Silence filled the air between us. Laughter from whatever game the children played floated through the small window near the ceiling behind Anna's sturdy bed. My lips twitched in response.

When Joseph and my brothers had left for Jerusalem, I chided myself for not accompanying him. Now, I realized staying behind with my sister and the children had been a good decision. They needed time to play and travel was hard on everyone. The cousins loved spending time together. Soon, Cleopas, recently promoted to vineyard steward, would move his family closer to Capernaum. What a different life my sister and her children would lead.

"Nomi is unwell." Anna's voice drew my attention away from the window and to her wrinkled visage. "I don't know if she will survive the pregnancy."

"The first is difficult for most women." I didn't want to encourage the woman's negativity. How difficult must it be for Nomi to live with a mother-in-law who disapproved of her? I knew exactly how harsh Anna's wrath could be.

"Was it difficult for you?"

Anna's dark eyes glared at me. It was a chance for her to throw my infidelity back into my face. Father had never told her about the angel of the Lord. Instead, she assumed I had consummated my marriage to Joseph before the ceremony took place. She wasn't the only one; everyone in Nazareth suspected the same.

"I would have preferred to be with family," I said.

Silently, I beseeched Jehovah for a special measure of patience. "But Joseph's aunt was an experienced midwife."

Anna stared at me a few moments longer. "Is there something you can do to encourage her to get out of bed? I fear her lethargy will make her too weak when her hour comes."

My narrowed eyes studied this woman seated before me. She had been a kind grandmother to my sons, although she hadn't paid much attention to Rachel. Her only daughter, Sarah, had died of an illness when she was but a babe. I had wept openly for my half-sister, but Anna shut herself away for several weeks. When she emerged from her mourning, her tolerance for my sister and I seemed even more forced.

I patted Rachel's back, staring at her chubby face, lips pursed in a sucking motion even as she slept. *Thank you, Jehovah, that Joseph loves his daughter as much as his sons. He is so much like my own father.*

"That's all."

I rose, dismissed from Anna's presence. I turned and left the room, pushing aside the skin into the bedroom where my sister-in-law reclined against a stack of straw pillows. Her face, pale and drawn, relaxed when I entered. Thankful it wasn't Anna? Likely.

"Thank you for coming, Mary."

I stepped forward and grasped her hands. They were cold. I leaned down and kissed her cheek.

"Rachel?" She held her arms out when I stood up.

I asked about her routines, while I untied the scarf holding Rachel to my breast. A smile transformed Nomi's features once I settled the baby in her arms.

"She's beautiful." Her tone was reverent.

I blushed at the comment. Most women didn't make a fuss over the appearance of daughters. After all, sons were what men coveted.

"I want mine to be a girl," Nomi said in a quieter tone. "I know Jesse needs a son, but girls will spend more time with their mother. It would be nice to have company around the house."

What she didn't say hung between us. Anna didn't offer to spend time with Nomi, help her with household chores, or offer any sort of support.

My heart constricted. What a terrible position Nomi was in. But there was no help for it. Jesse was the oldest son, responsible for our stepmother's welfare until she passed into the next life.

"The boys are good helpers," I said. "Jesus works in the shop with Joseph. Soon, Judah will be six, old enough for lessons at the synagogue. I'm sure Joseph will want to begin teaching him some things."

We visited for a while. Rachel awoke. I carried her back to the main room, changing her and feeding her behind the drape of the sleeping area I had used for thirteen years. Mary and I would sleep here with our children tonight. Would we stay with Nomi the entire week until the men returned from Jerusalem?

I thought of my small room and firm bed. The boys often slept with me when Joseph traveled. I would have Rachel to keep me company for sure.

Perhaps Nomi was right. Having a daughter might be a special blessing.

A squall from outside brought my head up. The curtain

jerked aside. My James rushed in, tears rolling down his face, streaking the dust with rivers of mud.

"Mahlon stepped on me," he said.

I laid Rachel over my lap, holding my hands out to my son. He hugged my shoulders, snuffling into the shawl draped across my body to provide modesty while I fed the baby.

"You are a strong carpenter, James," I soothed, patting his back. "Think of Father hitting his thumb with a hammer. Does he cry?"

James rubbed his head from side to side on my shawl. I bit back a smile when I thought of the smudges he would leave behind. Already, he rarely came to me for comfort. As much as I missed his warm hugs, I must continue teaching him to be a strong man.

The curtain fluttered. I looked up to see Jesus peeking in.

"Come, James. Mother is busy with Rachel."

"I am never too busy to share your hurts," I said, patting James again.

He pulled away. The dirt was smeared across his face, part of one cheek wiped clean. I ran my fingers through his thick, brown hair, still soft but getting so much longer.

I glanced up at Jesus, nodding. He stepped forward and gently turned James away.

"They are trying to hit the gate with pebbles now," Jesus said. "Do you think you can throw that far?"

James wiped a sleeve over his face, nodding vigorously.

Jesus is a wonderful son, Jehovah. You have blessed me beyond measure.

JERUSALEM - NISAN

MY TWENTY-SIXTH YEAR

*a*mong mothers, I am the worst. What woman can say she left her child in a strange city? What's more horrifying? I didn't even notice.

Joseph took both Jesus and Judah with him to make the sacrifice for Pesach, even though I argued that eight was much too young to witness so much blood. And why should he if he couldn't understand the significance?

Joseph acknowledged my objections with a nod and took his two oldest sons into the temple proper. I remained outside, seated in the shade of the courtyard walls.

After six pregnancies, I thought this time would be even easier than Joses. I missed my little man, left behind with Rachel and Simon to keep Nomi company at the farm. She had only one child, and he was always too weak to travel. Perhaps I should have listened to Joseph's suggestion to stay behind with the younger ones. My due date, still two months off, loomed over us.

I had been farther along when we traveled to Bethlehem, I argued. We were much younger then. Did I need him to remind me?

His hair and beard, mostly gray now, related the passage of years better than the collection of wrinkles at the corners of my eyes. When had twenty-six years seemed like a lifetime?

James played in the dirt while I reclined against the brick wall. Sweat beaded my forehead even in the shade. Nisan usually didn't affect me this way. Where were the cooling breezes? In the press of people coming to celebrate the feast, the heat was more oppressive than midday during Av.

In the morning, we would return to Nazareth. The thought relieved me. I couldn't understand how my cousin enjoyed living here. Perhaps it was different when no holy feast days were being celebrated.

Judah clutched the side of Joseph's robe. Behind him, Jesus scanned the crowds, exuding serenity. Nothing ruffled my firstborn son.

"I have a foot," Judah said, holding his hand out toward me. He unfolded grimy fingers in need of a wash to reveal an incredibly tiny hoof.

My stomach lurched, but I made my lips form a smile. I curled his fingers over the prized possession, grateful when it faded from view.

"There was so much blood," Judah said. "It smelled worse than the butcher shop and tannery."

Rolling in my midsection caused me to arch my back. I kept my fingers twined in his feathery brown hair.

"It is done," Joseph said, stepping beside me. His hazel eyes darkened, filled with concern for me.

I leaned into his arm when he rested his palm on my shoulder. Pounding behind my eyes blurred my vision.

"Mother is tired," Jesus said.

When I opened my eyes, his youthful visage hovered in front of me. His hand touched my brow, and a wave of energy passed through me, invigorating me. I smiled, tears of gratitude glistening in my eyes. He withdrew his hand from my face, and I missed the gentle pressure.

"I can carry the lamb," James said, rising from the ground, dust dripping from his fingers.

"Thank you, son," Joseph said. "I believe I will take care of it today."

"I already asked," Judah said, widening his eyes at his younger brother.

"You got to go in the temple," James said.

"Who will help Mother?" Joseph knew exactly how to get our competitive sons to do what he wanted.

Judah bolted in front of Jesus and wrapped his hands around my upper arm. His head would be even with my shoulder soon. They grew so fast.

James rested his fingers beneath my other elbow. His innocent smile sparkled in his dust-covered face. Who could resist returning it?

"Such strong helpers," I told them, smiling at each one.

Jesus stepped back when I rose to my feet. His eyes followed my progress. His concern mimicked Joseph's. His actions were so like the man who was not his father, although they looked nothing alike.

Jesus had wider, plainer features. Joseph's strong chin and chiseled cheekbones made him worthy of a second glance.

Eyes would pass over my firstborn—nothing more than an ordinary Jewish face. He was beautiful to me, but what else would a mother say?

Joseph's hand rested in the middle of my back for a few steps. When he took the lead, Jesus fell behind. I didn't see him again after that, so focused on keeping dust from my face and sunlight from my eyes. What a selfish woman I am!

Now, I worried my lip between my teeth and fought to keep the tears at bay. Emotions swirled in my stomach, chest and head.

I guessed the baby in my womb must be a girl. My emotions simmered in much the same way when I carried Rachel. Of course, I had never left any of my children behind in the capital city during that pregnancy, either.

"We will return tomorrow," Joseph said.

His hand rubbed my lower back as he knelt beside the cushion I had claimed as soon as the caravan stopped traveling for the day. Ten miles had never felt so far. Throbbing in my feet radiated up my calves and lashed against my knees. The ache in my back relented but little beneath my husband's ministrations.

"How will we find him? The city is huge. So many pilgrims."

"Jehovah will guide us."

Jehovah. Of course. I shouldn't be worrying over my son. I should be praying. After all, this boy held special importance in the mind of the Lord.

More tears burned my eyes and traced a pattern down my cheeks. The Lord had entrusted the boy to me, and my failure couldn't be more complete.

Joseph leaned his forehead against mine. Mary turned away, granting us space since privacy could never be acquired among such a throng of travelers. He whispered a petition, his warm breath tickling my ear and neck. Whether from the prayer or the intimacy, my heart settled into a steady rhythm.

Tomorrow we would retrace our steps. We would find Jesus.

ON THE SECOND day of searching, we thought about the temple. It should have been the first place we looked. After all, it was the last place I remembered seeing Jesus.

With the feast past, the crowds entering the temple were diminished. Where would a young boy have access? Would he be praying?

"I have never heard anything like it," a man said, pushing his way past us.

His clean, bright robes marked him as a nobleman or merchant. The man he spoke with was shorter but dressed as richly. I pressed myself into Joseph's side so they could pass.

"Who is he?"

"I never saw him before yesterday. This is the third day he's been teaching here."

"Seems young to know so much."

"That's why everyone keeps coming back to hear him."

Their words made my heartbeat quicken. Someone young had been teaching in the temple for three days. Jesus had been missing for three days. Twelve years was young, even though it was the cusp of manhood in synagogue services.

My eyes met Joseph's in the dim passageway between rooms. I could tell he was thinking the same thing: it sounded like Jesus was here.

An arched doorway opened into a larger room. Men stood in a loose circle around others who sat on benches. Every man on the benches held some sort of scroll. Some parchment contained words, while others were in the process of being etched by the scribe-driven quills. Most eyes focused on the center of the group. On a small stone pedestal, a boy sat cross-legged, motioning with his hands, an earnest expression on his face.

In those surroundings, he looked so much older, and it took a moment for me to recognize Jesus. Beside him, a man four times his age nodded agreement. All eyes were riveted on my son.

A spasm in my chest announced my relief. I sagged against Joseph's arm. He wrapped it around my waist and held me firmly to his side. His eyes scanned the room and rested on Jesus. A muscle in his cheek jumped, but otherwise his expression remained neutral.

Inside my own heart, anger nipped on the heels of the abating worry. Never before had Jesus defied us. I could not recall a single instance when he hadn't quickly obeyed any command we gave him. Even when he was Simon or Joses' age, he didn't whine or complain. Why would such a perfect son disappear without telling us?

I stepped away from Joseph. His hand remained on my elbow. Pushing my way through the circle of men, I fixed my stare on my firstborn. The hum of voices in the room stopped. Every eye studied me. Looking back, I realize I was the only woman in that room. I probably shouldn't even have been permitted inside its doors.

"Son," I said, drawing Jesus' attention from the old lawyer he spoke with, "why has thou thus dealt with us?"[1][xxix]

My voice shook. From nerves or aggravation? I don't know, but my question garnered a wave of whispered comments and caused looks to be exchanged in the gallery.

Joseph's hand squeezed my arm. I wanted to believe he was lending me strength, but, knowing him, he was likely warning me away from a confrontation. He traveled the path of least resistance, even if it meant going miles out of his way to avoid conflict.

Jesus' wide brown eyes brushed over my face and Joseph's. They held no apology or sorrow. A sort of energy emanated from him that I had never witnessed before. Not when he worked with wood. Not when he recited scripture with his brothers. Not when he sang psalms.

"Thy father and I have sought thee sorrowing."

"He's been here three days," someone beside me whispered.

I didn't turn. A blush crept into my face. I wouldn't let my own failures color this conversation.

"How is it that ye sought me?"[2][xxx]Jesus asked.

He unfolded his legs and stood up. The crowd of rabbis around him groaned in displeasure but moved aside so he could approach us.

With his hand, he gestured to the walls of the temple. "Wist ye not that I must be about my Father's business?"[3][xxxi]

"My business is in Nazareth, son," Joseph said.

Jesus glanced toward Joseph. Then his brown eyes stared into mine. The import of his words resonated inside my head and heart.

At the time, my emotions overwhelmed my ability to understand the implications. I was a worried mother, reacting with too much emotion. Later, I would more deeply consider his words. Even the awed responses of the learned men in the room would replay in my mind for days to come.

I held out my hand to him. He bowed his head slightly and took my arm. This was the Jesus I knew, the one who meekly followed our instructions.

As one, the three of us turned and walked away. Behind us, conversation rumbled and swelled, the discussion of the scriptures continuing as if we had never been there.

NAZARETH - TISHREI

MY THIRTY-SECOND YEAR

*D*arkness crowded around the straw mattress. The doctored wine sloshed in the cup I held, proof my hands felt as shaken by the moment as the rest of me. Another cough rattled Joseph's chest. Like a thousand cactus spines, the vibrations pierced my arm, which stretched behind his back.

Candlelight puddled from the table behind the circle of family. The light burned his eyes, Joseph said.

"Drink." His hoarse whisper grated along my heartstrings.

I held the cup to his flaky lips. Hollows around his eyes made them appear black, sunken. Ash in a cold fireplace had more color than his face—except for the ruddy circles indicating the fever still burned inside him. Not long for this world, the apothecary said when he delivered the packet of herbs to mix with the wine. The concoction eased the pain and fever, loosened the constriction in her husband's chest, and treated the symptoms. But the*schachepheth*[lxxxii] could not be stopped or cured.

My fingers gripped the pottery until I feared either it or they might shatter. I rubbed the center of my husband's back, while he took shuddering breaths. Finally, he leaned against me, his shoulder blades rising like mountain peaks beneath the linen tunic covering them.

"I will meet Father Abraham soon," Joseph said, his deep voice gaining strength. "It is time to bless my children."

I glanced up, noting my youngest daughter clinging to Jesus' side, her face hidden in the fold of his robe. I knew it was hard for her. She was not quite eight years old and watching her father die from disease. Jesus stood behind the others, his face in shadow.

"My son." Joseph held his hand out toward Judah.

Judah craned his neck, staring at his older brother. Jesus shook his head slightly.

After their silent communication, Judah stepped forward and knelt beside the low frame of the bed—my marriage bed, now situated in the main room of the house.

"Father, Jesus should go first."

Joseph acted as if he hadn't heard, his large, work-worn hand resting on Judah's forehead.

"I bless you, Judah." Joseph cleared his throat. "Your birth marked a happy time for your mother and I. Live to honor us before the Lord God."

After a brief silence, Judah stood and moved aside, allowing James to step closer to the bed. Through the tears I couldn't suppress, I saw Judah lean toward Jesus. With a shake of his head, Jesus silenced his brother, but he couldn't have missed the huge question marking Judah's countenance.

James knelt beside his father's outstretched hand, clearing his throat. Joseph settled his fingers into the curls rioting atop James' head.

"I bless you, James. Your heart is tender toward the world around you. Be a vessel of honor to our Lord God." A cough punctuated his words.

James looked up, tears streaking his face and whispered, "I will, Father," before standing, leaning on his brother Simon who had moved into position behind him.

Jehovah, please don't let his heart break over this loss. Show us how to comfort one another.

Simon knelt at Joseph's side, while James shuffled behind Judah and Jesus.

"My son, Simon, I bless your desire to learn a trade other than mine. You will find a place with Cousin Nadab in Bethlehem."

"Thank you, Father," Simon said. His voice shook nearly as much as the hand of his father resting on his head.

Joseph licked his dry lips. I held the cup for him again, noting it was halfway empty. Soon, I would need to heat more wine to dissolve another pinch of herbs.

Joses knelt beside his father, while I pressed the cloth to Joseph's brow. My husband rolled his head side to side, closing his eyes while a rattling exhale relaxed his shoulders.

Joseph reached out and rested his palm on the forehead of our youngest son, his namesake. His lips tilted slightly, and I imagined him reflecting on the energy of the boy, soon to be twelve. Joses, more than the others, mimicked his father, shadowing his moves and openly claiming his desire to be exactly like him.

Jehovah, my soul grieves for this one, who will reach manhood without the full guidance of his father. Stay near him, Lord.

"My youngest son, my name-bearer. Follow your heart to become the best carpenter in all of Galilee. The God of Abraham bless and keep you."

"No one is a better builder than you, Father," Joses said, looking up as his father's hand dropped back onto the woolen blanket covering his lower body.

Joses stood, hugging his sister Rachel. They were close in age—just a year apart—but their bond went deeper. His shoulders shook, and she patted him on the back. They were the same height, but I knew he would grow taller soon, like his older brothers.

Lord, keep her near Joses when she marries. They are good for each other.

All of our children shifted, turning to look at Jesus. Even Abigail poked her tear-stained face out, tilting it upward. Yet, Jesus didn't move forward.

I furrowed my brow, glancing toward my firstborn. My hands ministered to Joseph, dabbing his forehead and cheeks with the damp cloth, no longer very cool.

A strange air of expectation mingled with the whispers of my children. Joseph sipped at the wine, his hazel gaze connecting with mine as he finished. Those eyes, so mysterious when we had first married, spoke of love and loyalty now. All the words he would never say stared back at me, echoed by his tender provision.

I smiled at him. Did my look proclaim even a fraction of the emotion bubbling inside me? I couldn't know, but I hoped it did. He was my perfect match. My father had chosen well.

"I would bless my daughters," Joseph said, looking beyond me to the milling clench of bodies.

"But Jesus—" Judah's voice cut off as soon as Joseph raised his hand.

"Rachel," my husband called.

My oldest daughter wiped at her cheeks with the edge of her shawl, which had fallen to her shoulders when she embraced Joses. Her brown hair fell forward, veiling her flushed cheeks, as she knelt beside the bed.

Joseph's hand shook as he placed it on the crown of her head.

"Fairest Rachel, I bless you in the name of the Almighty God. May you be fruitful and faithful, well-loved by your husband, as was your namesake."

His hand brushed over the curtain of her hair before resting on his stomach. Jesus stepped forward, offering his hand to Rachel, who clung to him like a lifeline. His other hand nudged little Abigail toward the bed.

Our youngest daughter stumbled and fell to her knees. She scooted forward, her face toward the ground.

Joseph smiled again as he placed his hand on her head. "A blessing you have been to this house, Abigail, and a blessing of joy may you be to the hearth of your husband and the quiver full of children our Lord God endows upon you."

His voice broke. I reached forward, holding the cup for him. His eyes seemed even darker, the eyelids heavy. The medicinal herbs were making him sleepy. I brushed his hair off his forehead and glanced toward Jesus. His sisters clung to his sides. He gently pulled their arms away. James stepped forward to hold Abigail, and Rachel leaned into Joses.

Jesus knelt beside the bed. A soft beard outlined his jaw. Sorrow swam in his brown eyes. My breath caught in my throat.

Oh, Lord, I need your strength. I wondered if this was the soul-piercing sword old Simeon had spoken of so many years before.

Jesus stared into Joseph's rheumy gaze before flicking somber eyes toward me. I bowed my head so he wouldn't see the tears seeping from the corners of my own eyes.

Joseph touched Jesus' forehead, and Jesus bowed his head.

"The Lord has blessed you, firstborn of this house." Joseph coughed, wiping the corner of his mouth with his other hand. I reached forward with the cloth, but his attention was focused on Jesus.

"You are patriarch now. May the wisdom of the Almighty guide you in choosing the best futures for those yet unspoken for. His Spirit rests upon you, always."

The patriarchal blessing. I remembered my father passing it to Jesse. These were the words a son longed to hear from his father.

"Go with God," Jesus said, his tender gaze fixed on Joseph's face.

Joseph's eyes slid closed. His shallow breaths announced his slumber. The rattling and wheezing lessened when I lowered him flat onto the mattress. Abigail and Rachel stepped forward to pull his blankets higher.

Jesus strode through the stuffy room and out the door. The slat of light when he opened the door brightened the room without lifting the gloom. Judah followed on his heels, even though both James and Simon tried to hold him back.

None of them understood what I have often forgotten. Jesus is my firstborn son, but he is not of Joseph's flesh. Judah is the firstborn of Joseph. Should he have inherited the patriarchal blessing?

Oh Lord, my God, everything changed today. I will bury my husband, but somehow life will march onward. Be the father my children need, Lord. I am just a feeble mother, your handmaid still.

CANA - ADAR

MY FORTY-THIRD YEAR

For a moment, the cramping in my lower back and the salt stinging my eyes made me wish I hadn't volunteered to assist with this wedding feast for my sister's youngest daughter. Reflecting on it now, I know my part in the event was but a piece in the larger picture Jehovah painted. He is so gracious to continue allowing my presence in His masterpiece.

Cana, a village larger than Nazareth, is situated five miles closer to the Sea of Galilee than our home. Abigail and I had walked the distance over a week ago. My last unmarried daughter strolled the market with me, securing the ingredients necessary for the traditional wedding dishes: grapevine leaves, sardines, duck, mint, horseradish, and an assortment of fruits and melons. Each day became hotter than the last.

The bridegroom's villa was the largest home I had ever visited, even grander than the six-room gated home where my sister lived.

I spent most of the week cooking in the open kitchen. Fortunately, the wealthy groom had hired an abundance of servants so my sister, myself, and Abigail didn't have to make all the preparations for the expected crowd on our own.

James and Judah arrived together, both greeting me with a kiss on either cheek. Behind the respect, I saw anxiety in Judah. He desired a bride, but, since Jesus left, he has become responsible for my care.

I whispered to him as his rough beard scratched my cheek, "Having another woman in the house would be welcome to my old bones."

"You are not old, Mother," he told me, light sparkling in his eyes for the first time in forty days.

The feast was in full swing when I noticed a dust-covered group of men enter at the back of the canopy covering the villa's expansive courtyard. Wooden tables with rough benches scraped against the hand-hewn rock tiles. A group of younger men slid away from the newcomers. When I approached, the overwhelming odor of fish and seawater explained the wrinkled noses and covered faces.

In the midst of the four fishermen, two I recognized as sons of my cousin Salome, I saw Jesus. Across from him, a well-dressed man asked a question about some prophecy. Not that I listened. I noticed the sagging brown skin beneath my firstborn son's eyes and the matted hair against his scalp. The bones on his face stood out, and he looked as if he hadn't eaten in weeks. Why wasn't he taking better care of himself? Where had he been all this time?

"Thank you for attending your cousin's wedding." I leaned close to Jesus, pouring wine into the stone goblet on the table before him. The pitcher in my hand seemed to grow heavier as I served him.

"Of course, Mother," he said. His eyes, dark brown and filled with a depth of compassion I have never understood, fixed on mine.

His square face held no familial resemblance, except eyes and hair that matched mine in color. The weariness etched in every fine line tugged at my heart. Thirty years I had been the mother of this one, and each year made him more mysterious.

"Cousin Mary." Salome's oldest son, James, bowed his head toward me.

I filled his goblet. His younger brother, John, still a ruddy youth, no more than sixteen, stood and kissed both of my cheeks, his boyish face soft against mine.

"Thank you for inviting us," he said, watching my face while I poured his drink. "All the road dust isn't completely unwelcome, I hope? That's why we chose to sit in the court-yard instead of seeking my father in the house."

"We are honored by your acceptance." I didn't acknowl-edge the group of men who moved farther away, scowling and covering their noses.

"Don't tell Mother we didn't clean up before coming." James' voice boomed, even in the open air. "She is not half so forgiving as you."

I shook my head and returned to the makeshift kitchen, where I could oversee distribution of the next course. Perhaps I could find a moment to speak with Jesus later. I wanted to know why he had disappeared, since explaining to me would be a gentler path than facing his brothers. My shoulders slumped. Thankfully, they were seated in the hall, closer to their cousin's new husband.

The sun marched across the sky. The platters of food depleted as I directed servants to disperse it to the guests: the governor first, the bridegroom, and then by table according to their placement near the honored guests.

I reclined near the well at the back of the serving area, not really tasting the bread-wrapped mutton I chewed. Weariness pressed against my forehead. My arms weighed more than my shoulders could carry. Throbbing in my feet morphed into a steady ache.

"There is no more," one of the maids cried.

I glanced up to see the bridegroom's steward standing amid a bevy of servants. None of them would meet his gaze. The young woman who spoke, one of the best servers during this event, pressed her lips together. In the waning sunlight, I thought I saw tears glistening on her eyelashes. She ducked her head, so I couldn't say for certain.

Gritting back a groan of protest, I stood and hurried to the steward's side.

"Is there a problem?"

The man's gray eyes slashed across me. His clean-shaven face, lighter than those around him, announced his non-Jewish heritage. I leaned away from him and dropped my gaze to his chin.

"The governor calls for more wine. These servants tell me there is none."

"We had the casks stored in the cellar," I told him. "Check beneath the stairs," I said to a young man standing nearby. He turned to do my bidding.

"I have checked twice, Mistress Mary," the maid said. "They are all used up. We have no wine."

"Unacceptable," the steward said. His eyes cut into me again, narrowing. "Weren't you in charge of securing the proper amounts?"

"I can run to the wine seller," one of the other young men volunteered.

"That would be subpar vintage for sure," the steward said.

"Everyone is well-drunk," said an older servant. "They will hardly taste whatever we serve them."

The steward's knifelike gaze pierced the old man. "You would shame my master in this way?"

"I will take care of it," I said.

Everyone stared at me. I brushed past the steward whose glare pushed me to step briskly. He would not have me or the servants to blame for this shortage. The staff deserved commendation for their tireless service at this never-ending event.

I stopped behind the bench where Jesus sat. He sopped a crust of bread along his plate, listening to the well-dressed man across from him.

I moved closer, until my hip rested against Jesus' shoulder. Several men glanced up at me. One of them lifted his goblet, as if I was there to serve him.

"They have no wine," I said.

The goblet clattered onto the table.

"Is the feast over?"

"The party has been running longer than we expected," said one of the fishermen.

I stood beside my son, placing my hand at the base of his neck. A sense of calm shuddered through me. I took a deep breath.

He turned his face toward me, waiting.

"They have no wine,"[1][xxxiii] I repeated.

After thirty years of motherhood, I knew how to project meaning into a glance. He could hear my unspoken words: "You need to do something about this." I wouldn't embarrass him by treating him like a child in front of his companions.

"Woman," he said without inflection, "what have I to do with thee?"[2][xxxiv]

I continued giving him the maternal stare. This was my problem, and I needed his help. Had I asked him to show special favor to me before? Never. Only the respect and honor a mother deserved. This was different. A crowd of innocent servants would suffer chastisement if he chose to ignore my pleas.

He sighed, his shoulders lifting and falling beneath the palm of my hand.

"Mine hour is not yet come."

In my son's dark eyes I saw his acquiescence to my silent plea. Turning away, I hustled back to the crowd of distraught servants. The man I had sent to the cellar stood with head bowed being lashed by the steward's tongue.

"Come with me." I gestured to the servants. The steward's glare meant nothing to me now. "I have found a solution to our beverage shortage."

Half a dozen men and women followed me back to Jesus' table.

I pointed to my son. "Whatsoever he saith unto you, do it."[3][xxxv]

They exchanged startled looks amongst themselves. I stepped back, waiting for the command. What would he do? How would my firstborn son solve this problem?

Jesus gestured toward the wall of the villa. A collection of stone water pots, half-shaded from the waning sunlight, were shoved against the wall. Guests used these huge jugs to wash before entering the festivities.

"Fill the water pots with water,"[4][xxxvi] he told the servants.

Surprise rippled through the huddled servers. When they glanced at me, I nodded, keeping a stern set to my mouth. He wouldn't serve the guests water, especially not from those wash pots. Water needed to be purified, and even then, the sediment made it less than palatable.

Scurrying like well-trained servants do, each of them chose a water pot from beside the wall and disappeared around the house toward the well. I wondered if they whispered about the odd command to each other. Would the steward waylay them?

About the time I feared I would have to retrieve them, the line of six servants emerged. The water pots sat on the shoulders of the men and on the heads of the women. Moisture dripped down the sides, leaving a trail of dots in their wake.

When all of them stood beside me, Jesus turned toward us. His dark gaze touched each pot of water, as if he counted them. With a slight nod, he said, "Draw out now, and bear unto the governor of the feast."[5][xxxvii] The servants stared at me with wide eyes.

"Did you hear him?" I asked.

The faces of the servants fell. They believed their doom was upon them.

The maid who had incurred the wrath of the steward turned toward the serving area. With trepidation, the others followed.

I turned toward Jesus, intending to thank him. He had already returned to his nearly empty plate.

"Water for the governor?" a brash fisherman said. "I'm almost willing to endure the stuffy hall to see it."

"After this, you will have more faith," Jesus said to the man.

I brushed my hand against his shoulder and turned toward the villa. I wanted to witness this firsthand. I didn't need to improve my faith in my son. I had known of his uniqueness for more than thirty years. Still, I wondered how he had rescued the servants and my sister's reputation.

The serving girl held a pitcher in each hand. She poured the wine into the governor's goblet, a silver affair with swirling designs etched on the sides.

He lifted the cup to his lips. The maid paused, waiting for his reaction before pouring wine into the groom's father's waiting cup. I stepped closer, tuning out the conversation swelling around me.

Surprise flashed on the governor's face. He took another sip of wine, savored it. The knot of flesh on his throat bobbed when he swallowed. He stood, raising his cup toward the host.

"Every man doth set out the best wine at the beginning," he said. The bridegroom stared up at him, his own cup raised partway to his mouth. "Thou has kept the good wine until now."6xxxviii

After taking another swallow, the governor sat down, holding his cup toward the maid. She ducked her head and refilled it. She poured wine for everyone at the honored table before her pitchers were empty.

"A miracle," she whispered to me on her way to replenish the pitchers.

It was the first miracle Jesus performed, but it would not be the last.

CAPERNAUM - NISAN

MY FORTY-FOURTH YEAR

"What is he doing with those men?"

I bowed my head, holding the veil over my mouth. Judah asked the same question of James at least once every hour.

I stared ahead. The fishermen and others who sat with Jesus at the marriage feast encircled him, asking questions as they walked. Dust stirred around their feet, nearly choking me when I walked through the cloud several paces behind them, on the heels of my sons.

"He should be returning with us. He has responsibilities."

Abigail wrinkled her nose. "Now you have those responsibilities." She coughed, and I patted her hand.

Judah huffed, clenching his short, calloused fingers into fists.

"We will finish the betrothal agreement with Reuven for Abigail, and you can return to Nazareth." James wiped his hand over his brow while he spoke.

"Pesach is in ten days," Judah said.

"Yes, brother," James said.

I narrowed my eyes at my second son. Judah needed to speak frankly with Jesus rather than take his frustration out on his family. James worked hard and shouldn't be punished because of Judah's anger. James had left Nazareth years ago to work in Tiberias and on other construction projects Herod commissioned. Soon, he would barter for his own wife, and it was only fair that his older brother married first.

But Jesus would not marry. He had told me that several months ago when I mentioned Judah's interest in the rabbi's daughter. Jesus informed me that Judah was free to make his own betrothal agreement, and there would be no offense taken.

Judah nodded when I passed along this information, but he hadn't set up any meetings with Rabbi Yael to discuss a betrothal. I didn't understand his delay.

"Will we see Cousin Salome while we're here?" Abigail asked.

I nodded, expecting my cousin would be glad to receive us.

"Those other fishermen, sons of Jonas"—James gestured to the group surrounding Jesus—"are Zebedee's partners."

"They weren't invited to the wedding," Judah said. His scowl made his eyebrows press together until they resembled a thick caterpillar on his forehead. "Crass fishermen, showed up for free food and drink."

Abigail gasped.

I gripped Judah's wrist as his arm swung backward with

his natural stride. "Your cousins are fishermen and are wealthier than our family."

Judah glared at me. Usually he had warm, expressive eyes, deep brown like my own. Now, they gave me a chill.

"You shouldn't degrade their profession," I finished.

"Of course, Mother," he said, dropping his eyes to where my fingers clasped him. "I meant no disrespect."

I released him, but my heart sank beneath the dust encrusting my feet. For twenty-six years, I had tried to subdue his wrathful spirit, and still his temper caused his mouth to speak rashly.

When I glanced toward James, I saw a silent apology on his face. As always, he had a softer heart and keener perception. I dropped my gaze and silently prayed that Jehovah would teach my stubborn son those lessons that I could not. My influence on him lessened with each passing day.

The road widened, allowing for increased traffic. A cacophony of sound interrupted my meditations. Men called to each other. A herd of goats baaed, a dog yipping at their heels. Wheeled carts pulled by mules clattered and squealed.

Abigail pressed closely to my side, our shoulders rubbing. Her forehead glistened with perspiration. Once, she would have held me for security. At eighteen, old for a maiden bride, her clinginess was meant to keep me from getting lost in the throng.

The return to Nazareth couldn't happen soon enough. Judah was right, though, we would be traveling on to Jerusalem before too long. Even making good time, it would take four days to reach the city from Nazareth. Of course, the press for time might keep Judah moving forward with the contractual arrangements, instead of grousing about how Jesus should be handling them.

James might be a better choice to serve as patriarch. He held his emotions close, like his father. (Where had Judah learned his temper?) My third-born son dealt with the merchants more often than Judah and was more personable. Perhaps he could handle the negotiations with this merchant, even if the merchandise—so to speak—was his youngest sister. Not that it was proper for Judah to relegate the duty to his younger brother when he had embittered himself against Jesus for doing that very thing.

Ahead, the dome of the synagogue sparkled. Jesus and the men he called disciples approached it. They clustered in front of a smaller house pressed against the wall surrounding the house of worship.

Judah elbowed past the disciples standing between him and Jesus. John, younger but not smaller, halted him with a hand to the chest. Words were exchanged. John's unbearded face began to redden, clashing with his auburn hair. It wasn't going well.

Jesus turned, placing a hand on John's shoulders. His face, calm as always, remained unchanged as Judah railed on him. Again, the words couldn't be heard, but I knew how Judah's tongue cut when wielded by his lashing anger.

Jesus shook his head. Judah raised his hand, only to have John snatch his wrist and push him back a step. Another touch from Jesus and John withdrew, stepping slightly behind Jesus. My cousin's eyes smoldered with anger.

Judah turned back toward us, his face a storm cloud.

"Let's just go to Zebedee's," I said to James.

We turned away before Judah reached us.

"He's not coming," Judah announced, striding past Abigail and me as if we stood still.

"We can make the arrangements," James said.

"Shouldn't have to," Judah said. "It's Jesus' place as patriarch."

"Reuven seemed eager to reach an agreement when last I spoke with him," James said.

"I hope someone is willing to speak on my behalf," Abigail said.

Judah glanced at her, chastened. His face softened, and he ducked his chin. Both of my daughters had always known how to wrap their brothers around their fingers. I shook my head. Where did they learn that? It wasn't from me.

Later, we sat on cushions along the wall in the expansive atrium where Reuven received guests. His youngest son, guaranteed a partnership in the mercantile, cast glances toward Abigail. He was no more than twenty and reminded me of Joses. For a man, it was nearly unheard of to marry so young, but most girls were expecting a child by sixteen. Jesus had allowed Abigail to refuse the few suitors in Nazareth who approached him asking for a betrothal contract, and now she was old for a maiden bride.

Judah was right. Jesus should have already made an arrangement for his sister's future. Jesus had sat with Joseph during the bartering for Rachel's hand. He knew the intricacies. As the patriarch, it was his responsibility. For a moment, I justified Judah's indignation.

Then logic intervened. Judah would be responsible for

his own daughters someday. And more immediately, he needed to make his own arrangement with Rabbi Yael.

"Wist ye not that I must be about my Father's business?" The words of twelve-year-old Jesus sitting among the scribes and doctors in the temple echoed across my heart.

Joseph was not his father and being a carpenter wasn't his purpose in life. Why should I expect Judah to understand this?

While this bargaining was essential for Abigail's well-being, Jesus had a larger responsibility. Only now did I begin to see it would take him far away from home and family. A pinch in my heart made my breath catch.

"He's handsome," Abigail whispered in my ear, covering her mouth with a napkin.

The sparkling hazel eyes of my youngest child drew me back into the moment.

"Do you think he can grow a beard?" She pressed her lips in a tight line, but her eyes glowed with merriment.

"Maybe in five more years," I replied. The giggle that escaped before she clasped her hand over her mouth sent trills of pleasure through my stomach.

Just that quickly, my sweet daughter reminded me of one of motherhood's more pleasurable duties: sharing joy with a child. My heart swelled with happiness, and peace flooded my mind.

I shushed her behind the guise of fanning myself with the napkin. Her betrothed adjusted his position so he could stare at my beautiful daughter. She ducked her chin. Only I witnessed the blushing of the beautiful bride-to-be.

Across the room, James pandered to the merchant,

smoothing over Judah's curtness. My two sons made a good bargaining team. As I listened to the men, I realized James had already mentioned creating a partnership of sorts with the merchant. This included Reuven carrying a stock of tables in his mercantile as part of the bride price. For the first year, only the cost for supplies would return to the carpentry shop. The rest would build in trust for Abigail. After that time, a small percentage would continue to build for her, the shop would reap one-fourth of the profit, and the remainder would be for Reuven and his sons.

Judah seemed unwilling to commit to the number of tables Reuven desired each month. James agreed to return home and help Judah and Joses construct the first batch and deliver them to Reuven himself.

Reuven's youngest daughter knelt before me, proffering a tray laden with figs and sweetmeats. I had never been a fan of the rich fruit, but I took a smaller pastry to keep from offending the hostess. Without turning my head, I could feel her eyes resting on us. After Abigail plopped her own tart into her bowl, the girl returned to the men, offering them a second choice.

I considered the size of the gated compound. What a different world for my baby girl—aside from the size of the home, there were several servants that assisted with the service and cleanup of the meal.

The marriage contract provided only a separate room in this house for the married couple. Of course, for all I knew, that room could be as large as our home in Nazareth.

James had found an advantageous match for his sister.

Judah could be furious with Jesus, but his own younger brother had done most of the groundwork for this betrothal.

I sighed. Abigail glanced at me. She reached over and covered my hand with hers. It felt softer than normal. She had been rubbing olive oil into her skin during the trip from Cana.

"I will miss you too, Mother," she said. "Will you be too lonely with only Judah and Joses for company?"

I shook my head, placing my other hand atop hers and patting the back of her knuckles.

"Judah wants to take a wife."

"Rabbi Yael's daughter," Abigail said. "She seems too young for him."

"That is the way of things, daughter."

Abigail nodded, her eyes sparkling when she gazed into my face. "I'm glad I don't have to marry an old man."

Her words were barely more than a whisper, but I shushed her anyway.

Would her sunny disposition be welcome in this austere home? Other than James and Abigail's, I hadn't seen many smiles.

Jehovah, I choose to trust you with my youngest daughter. I will not worry about her well-being. She knows how to be a good wife. Guard her heart until they find love for one another.

Looking into the boy's face, turned toward us still, I could see his desire for Abigail. I took his adoration as assurance from God that all would be well.

PESACH - NISAN

MY FORTY-FOURTH YEAR

*P*eople clogged the streets. My shawl hardly protected my lungs from the constant swirl of dust mingled with the scent of animal dung. Abigail's fingers tightened around the bend in my elbow where she had hooked her arm through mine at the last mile post.

Abigail and I shuffled down a narrow street heading toward the older part of the city and my cousin's home. Susanna had married a member of the Sanhedrin and lived in a five-room house with a private courtyard. In the scope of Jerusalem's grandeur, it wasn't the house of a wealthy man, but it made the places I had called home seem shabby.

Chickens fluttered up when we turned sharply into an alley leading to Broad Street and Susanna's home. Both Abigail and I gasped when the squawking fowls crossed our path. She covered her face with her hands, dropping my arm in the process. I shook my head at her unreasonable fear of the noisy farm birds.

Abigail waved her arms at the clucking hoard, recovered from her sudden regression. I recalled the day when the little girl, carrying food scraps into her uncle's yard, had been accosted by a flock of hungry hens.

"Away, you smelly pests." She flailed her arms, dislodging her headdress.

"Perhaps we will have chicken for the pre-Pesach meal," I teased.

"As long as it is dead and well-cooked, I won't complain."

"Next year will be different," I said, a wave of melancholy washing away my smile. "You will celebrate the feast with his family." And, given their position in the community, it would be a more elaborate event than the humble offerings of a carpenter.

"I will still visit you at Cousin Susanna's house," she said, hooking her elbow through mine after straightening her shawl. Her pat on my forearm comforted me while making me feel childish. "They often travel here a week in advance. This year was different because of the betrothal meeting."

During the meeting, Abigail's espoused husband asked to waive the one-year waiting period. Could she be prepared in one month's time?

They agreed on three months, even though Judah scowled through the remainder of the evening. In the months since Jesus had left him in charge of the shop, his disposition had deteriorated from unpleasant to cranky to obnoxious. And it rubbed off on everyone in the house.

I must stop brooding.

Lord, may Judah find a forgiving spirit as he finds the unblemished sacrifice for Pesach. Turn his mind toward more important things. Like remembering your care and celebrating the deliverance of our forefathers from bondage.

The whitewashed gate clattered when Abigail knocked on it. A scrawny boy pulled it inward, and we drank in the sight of the fountain bubbling at the center of the courtyard. The water's tinkling melody reminded me how dust-covered my throat felt after the day's travel.

"Mary." My cousin stepped out from a darkened doorway leading to the inner rooms.

Her brown hair was wrapped in an intricate weaving of ropes interspersed with ribbons. I admired her light blue tunic, such a contrast from my dark-colored robes.

I leaned into her embrace, kissing her cheek as she kissed mine. An aroma befitting a bouquet of flowers rose from her skin. It lingered when she transferred her greeting to my daughter.

After Susanna handed our belongings to the boy, we followed her to a well-appointed greeting room. Plush cushions were shoved against every wall, circling a woven Egyptian cotton rug. A divan with a wooden frame sat opposite the doorway. Susanna excused herself to bring some refreshments from the kitchen, and Abigail, such a gracious girl, offered to help.

Once I sat down, my feet throbbed. I hadn't noticed their aching while we traveled. They needed a good rubdown, which would have to wait until we could wash up before the evening meal. Tomorrow would be the feast day. We would all travel to the temple for the sacrifice then purchase the herbs and root vegetables to accompany the meat for Seder. [lxxxix]

Sighing, I propped a smaller pillow behind my back and relaxed against the wall. Light from the central hallway illumined the room, but the whitewashed walls brightened it even further. I wondered if I could convince Judah to cover our interior walls with the wash. He probably wouldn't want to change anything without the approval of his future wife.

My eyes drifted closed. I started awake at the sound of Abigail's melodious laughter. She followed our cousin into the room. Both carried trays laden with food and drink. Susanna's tray had four short legs, and she situated it between the cushion I sat on and the one beside me.

"The games are so much fun, but I always knew Elijah wouldn't come for the supper," Abigail said, taking on the superior tone she'd learned from her older sister.

"I'm sure the boys must, as well. But it's so refreshing to have small children enjoying the feast with us."

I smiled and nodded when Susanna handed me a cup of juice. It had the tart aftertaste of an early season grape harvest but was watered down enough to keep my lips from puckering. It tasted nothing like the sweet, succulent wine Jesus had supplied at the wedding.

Abigail stood over me, fussing with my shawl. I noticed she was bareheaded, quickly making herself at home in our temporary quarters. I leaned forward so she could release the fabric that was trapped between my back and the wall. My flushed face immediately felt cooler.

I thanked her. She folded the garment and sat it on a cushion near the doorway. Susanna handed me a piece of bread coated with her signature bean and spice mixture and garnished with a dozen raisins. Something about drying out the grapes turned them sweeter than sugar.

I set my cup on the floor beside me and popped the treat in my mouth, resuming my place against the cushion.

Conversation about recent events in the family and the city entertained Abigail. She shared her experience at the betrothal meeting, and I shook my head as she freely admitted to her whispered shenanigans. Susanna met my eyes, and the understanding of mothers passed between us.

We heard the raised voices before we saw the men. Judah's voice echoed off the walls. I sighed, closing my eyes. Apparently the trip to get the sacrifice had done nothing but worsen his mood.

"I'm just glad Mother wasn't there to see it," Judah bellowed, stomping into the room. All the lightness and joy were sucked away.

He plopped onto the divan, reaching out toward Susanna, demanding a drink. She set her refreshments aside to pour juice for both of my sons.

James stood in the doorway, a kid slung around his neck. His stance and the set of his jaw reminded me of my father. Nostalgia tugged my heart.

"It should be fine in the courtyard, James," Susanna said, rising to her feet to show him where to put the goat. Its liquid brown eyes, so innocent, stared around the room.

Judah drained his cup. He held it toward his sister and grunted. My pleasant mood dispelled further at the sight.

"Show some manners," I scolded.

He turned to me, a different sort of flush coloring his neck. Abigail took the cup and refilled it.

"I would prefer wine," he said.

"I'm sure you'll have it with dinner." I hardly recognized the hard edge in my voice. I must have been wearier than I knew.

"What's gotten you stirred up now?" Abigail asked, settling onto the cushion to my right, facing the divan where Judah sat.

I chewed a few more raisins. Judah swilled the juice in his mouth before swallowing.

"Is that her mashed bean spread?"

Abigail spread some onto one of the flat rounds of unleavened bread and tossed a couple figs on top. She handed it to him, leaning forward on her knees rather than standing to deliver it. I shook my head at their antics. We weren't at home. At least no one was present to witness their inappropriate behavior.

"Maybe no wine if she's already serving unleavened bread," Judah mumbled. His bite devoured half the rolled-up chunk.

Susanna and James returned. His hair sparkled, wet from a recent dousing. Of course he would wash after handling the animal. I glared at Judah's dusty hands as he popped a fig in his mouth.

"The boys saw Jesus at the temple," Susanna said, pouring juice for James and handing it to him.

That explained Judah's ugly temper. My heart pinched inside my chest. I despised this division in our family. I was reminded again of Simeon's words: "a sword shall pierce through thy soul." Cold chills struck me at the memory.

"He was causing havoc," Judah said.

"What do you mean?" Abigail's eyes were wide.

"It's really a madhouse there before Pesach," James said.

"And he made it much worse." Judah leaned toward Susanna with an extended hand after she passed the bread and fruit to his brother. "Delicious, Cousin. Another?"

Her eyes widened, but she prepared another piece of bread for Mr. Demanding. I wished the pillow could swallow me whole and save me from the fiery shame licking up from the collar of my tunic.

"Are you talking about the commerce they've set up in the outer court?" Susanna held the jug of juice up toward each of us. We all shook our heads, and she placed it on the legged tray before sitting on the other end of Abigail's cushion.

"He said they were making the temple a den of thieves," James said.

Abigail gasped and clasped a hand over her mouth.

"That's not the worst of it," Judah said. He chewed another bite of bread, drawing out the suspense as long as possible.

I looked past him at James. His eyes studied the cup in his hand, as if he knew I wanted something from him, and he was avoiding it.

"He threw their tables over." Gasps all around greeted this statement. Judah smirked. "He had some sort of whip and he chased them out into the court of the Gentiles. That's when he called them thieves."

James shook his head. "That's not what he said. It was more like, 'My Father's house is a place of prayer, and you've changed it into a den of thieves.'"

Judah shrugged. "Same thing."

It wasn't the same thing at all, and he knew it. The ire bubbling in my stomach unsettled the raisins like pebbles in a rushing stream bed.

"Did you speak to him?" Susanna asked. She would want to know if he was going to sit the Pesach meal with us. I could answer that.

James shook his head. "Things were out of control. It would have taken hours to push through the crowd and reach him."

"Not that speaking to him changes anything," Judah muttered.

"It doesn't really sound like Jesus to me," Abigail said.

"He's gone crazy," Judah snapped. "You can't see it because you've worshiped him for years."

It was too much. He spoke rashly because of his anger, but I couldn't allow this disrespect to continue. Yahweh forbid! I bolted to my feet, wavering as blood pulsed in my ears.

"Enough!"

James stood, steadying me with a calloused hand on my shoulder. Judah's face blanched for a second before he stood, inches from me. The sweetness of the fruit mingled with the spices of the spread on his breath. Combined with the staleness of his sweat, the smell nearly gagged me.

"You need to face reality, Mother," he said. "Jesus was always the perfect one, but he's going astray now. Why won't you admit it?"

My hand acted of its own accord. The echoing smack of skin against skin surprised me. My audible gasp joined those from behind me. My palm stung, and red leeched into his cheek. Tears blurred my vision.

Judah stepped back. His words had been stopped, but his expression told the true story. Rage boiled beneath the surface. His teeth gritted, and, beneath the growing slash of red on his face, a muscle leaped like a wild hare.

James pulled me beneath his shoulder. I shuddered, burying my face against his rough robe.

"He's making a spectacle of himself everywhere he goes, Mother," Judah said. "You'll have to accept that sooner or later." He stormed away, swallowed by the dim hallway.

"I'm sorry, Mother," James said, patting my shoulder.

I wished he would say Judah didn't mean the things he said about Jesus, but he would never intentionally lie to me. And hadn't I started it all? By keeping the truth of Jesus' parentage to myself? It would help nothing to tell them now. It might even make the rift between brothers greater.

Abigail stood beside me. "Why don't I take you to our room?"

"You must be exhausted from the journey," Susanna said. "You need rest after the busy weeks you've had."

"I am tired," I said, sagging against Abigail.

James held my other arm to keep me from folding under the weight of my misdeeds. Losing my temper in the face of Judah's outburst was the worst thing I could have done. Jehovah forgive me. I needed to pray at the temple more desperately than ever before.

Tomorrow couldn't come soon enough.

~

CROWDS SWIRLED AROUND US. Shoulders shoved me into Abigial. Men parted from the crowd as their wives shuffled beside us into the women's court.

"It's worse since that Jesus of Nazareth threw the sellers out." The young man's dark beard was sparkling with beads of sweat.

"Hardly." The older woman whose arm he guided barely grunted her reply.

I cast my eyes to the ground. Two people with differing opinions about my son's actions. I didn't fully understand the repercussions, but I'd hoped for a quieter place to bare my heart to Yahweh. Isn't that what Jesus meant proclaiming the temple as a place of prayer?

Abigail leaned close. "Stop worrying, Mother."

She was right. I hugged her arm closer to my side. Worry was the opposite of faith. Could I expect Yahweh to hear my prayer if all I did was fret about what people thought about Jesus?

And why should it be different now? He'd begun his life on earth under the curse of being an ill-conceived child. Somehow, we'd born the scorn, and it hadn't affected the tenderness of his personality. What these strangers thought now wouldn't deter him from God's plan.

Yahweh, what is your plan?

Soon, Abigail and I stood among the muttering cluster of women. I closed my eyes and opened my heart to the Great God of Abraham.

It took several minutes before my regrets and anxieties flowed from my spirit into the calming heart of Jehovah.

Always He loved me. Always He listened to me. More, He *heard* me.

And in that moment, the pang of loneliness for my father and Joseph echoed through my heart. They had always loved and listened to me, as well. I missed that compassionate understanding, so free from judgment and condemnation.

Like Jesus offers everyone.

Yes, Yahweh. Thank you for reminding me. Jesus is the true representative of your understanding heart. Help the people to see that. Keep them from hatefulness.

I swallowed a ball of grief. *A sword shall pierce through your own soul,* the old priest's words pounded inside my skull. For a moment, I couldn't catch my breath and wavered against my daughter. Her arms tightened on mine, and I stilled.

Yahweh, make Abigail's marriage a happy one. Let love grow and bless her with many sons, and at least one loving daughter, one with a sweet spirit like hers.

Forgive Judah's anger. Show him how to forgive Jesus.

For what? The thought stopped my prayer, and I had to confess the surge of anger.

He doesn't understand Jesus' true purpose, Jehovah. I spoke to the angel, and I don't really understand. Give me more patience. Thank you for James, who is always a peacemaker. Help Judah to find a wife that will make him forget his bitterness.

After the prayers were finished, Abigail and I pressed through the crowds to the marketplace.

"He drove everyone out," a man said.

"He speaks with authority," said another.

The voices ran together like dirt and water. I blocked them out, focusing on Abigail's voice as we picked out the herbs and roots Susannah asked us to contribute for Sedar.

All was right between Yahweh and me, and even as the crowds surged around us, the tumult inside me faded away.

CAPERNAUM - AV

MY FORTY-FIFTH YEAR

*R*abbi Yael's daughter was a pretty little bird who loved to hear her own voice. Now this constant source of empty chatter had become my daughter. *Thank you, Lord, that she was unable to make this trip to Capernaum.*

In truth, I probably didn't need to accompany Judah either, but I never refused a chance to see Jesus or Abigail.

Judah's sole reason for the trip was to secure a shop for James in the city. It seemed the contractual arrangement with Abigail's new family had become a greater boon for their carpentry business than either had anticipated. James had found three prospective buildings in Capernaum for this new workshop. Always the dutiful one, he didn't want to commit to any of them without his brother's approval.

"As it should be," Judah said when he received the message from James.

The increase in business meant more money, which

translated into security for Judah's future bride and children. Wasn't that good news? But my son could never be satisfied.

Judah groused about the additional accounting work. "I'm a carpenter not a mathematician," he often said. Yet, when I offered to take a look at the accounts, he shoved my offer aside.

"I had my own business before I married," I told him. "Your grandfather taught his daughters to understand the economics of commerce alongside his sons." In fact, my brother Jesse often brought the records to me before he made any livestock sales or trades. Not that Judah would have listened if I had mentioned that fact.

"I'm taking care of you, Mother."

His incessant rub against his older brother. Poor Judah, forced to be the patriarch of a family that seemed to prosper with every passing year. No one dared ask him where he would be if Jesus were running the shop.

I pulled the edge of my shawl more tightly over my lower face to cover a sigh. A smattering of recent rains had settled much of the dust. Judah walked several paces in front of me, his father's staff leading out before every stride. Seeing it reminded me of so many other journeys when Joseph led the way.

"James will meet us at Reuven's store," Judah said. "You can visit with Abigail while we take care of business."

It would be nice to see Abigail. It had been a year since the wedding, and correspondence could be difficult to arrange in slower seasons of trade.

At the store, Abigail's husband beamed at the sight of me. He quickly offered to walk me around to the house. I noticed he still had only fine baby hair on his chin, which reminded me of sharing laughter with Abigail, and I smiled.

After greetings from the women of the house and enjoying a sip of watery grape juice, Abigail begged to show me her own rooms.

"As soon as he saves enough, we'll get our own place," Abigail said.

The room felt airy with a high window on one wall over-looking the garden at the rear of the complex. Several cushions, a chest I recognized as her brother's handiwork, and a simple rug decorated the outer room. A richly woven curtain divided the room. On the back side of it, a large fluffy mattress ("Feathers, Mother!") sat atop a wooden frame.

The bed frame had been a wedding gift from James and Joses. Judah refused to work on it, claiming their trade agreement was gift enough. Abigail's husband's family was getting the better end of that deal, after all. No one bothered to remind him that the first few years' profits that went mostly to Reuven were to establish a dowry for Abigail. It wouldn't have changed anything.

Yahweh, please soften my son's heart. I don't know this bitter man Judah has become. Please lead him back to you with a merciful hand.

Later in the afternoon, James knocked on the outer gate. When he entered, he refused any refreshments. "I've come for you, Mother," he said, offering me his hand so I could rise from the cushion where I reclined.

Abigail and I embraced. I whispered encouragement in her ear to belay her fears since she wasn't yet with child. Her smile brightened even though light reflected from the sheen of moisture in her eyes.

"Thank you, Mother." She kissed both of my cheeks, her flowery scent wafting over me.

Everyone would assume she thanked me for visiting, but I knew the truth. She was happy with her husband, but the pressure to bear him sons weighed on her heart. It was the Lord who opened the womb, I had assured her.

I returned her sweet kisses. Gone were the days I received those precious gifts on a daily basis.

After thanking her husband's mother, James and I departed. I expected to join Judah at the mercantile.

"Where is your brother?" I looped my arm through James' elbow as we moved into a more crowded street.

"Talking to Jesus."

I could have stumbled over my heart at that moment.

"Is that necessary? Wouldn't the owner accept a contract from Judah?"

James sighed. "It has nothing to do with the new shop. He wants to harangue Jesus about overseeing the expansion."

Would he never move past this resentment? Another prayer sprang to my lips (how many was that for my billy goat of a son today?): *Lord, please don't turn a deaf ear to the problem in Judah's soul. Forgive me, Lord. I know you hear my petitions, but how can you penetrate such a stubborn heart?*

A throng of people crowded the street ahead. They pressed against a building set on a slight rise. I recognized the insignia over the door of the larger building—a synagogue. The door to the smaller house stood open and everyone leaned toward it. We'd been here before. It was the home of Simon bar Jonas.

Judah stood on the edge of the crowd, arms crossed over his chest. Surely, he didn't mean to fight through this mob to talk to his brother?

He motioned to us, and we went to stand beside him, James keeping his arm over my shoulders to protect me from the constant jostling.

Judah gestured to a small boy in the crowd—maybe six years of age. He squatted down in front of the child and offered him a penny if he would go in and bring one of Jesus' followers out.

"Will you recognize them?" James asked.

The boy nodded, eyes wide as he studied the coin. He reached out to take it, but Judah clasped his hand over it.

"When you return with one of the twelve he travels with."

The child had no trouble weaving his way through the crowd. A few men pulled their money purses out of his reach, but no one stopped him. Soon, he disappeared inside the house. I leaned against James.

"Do you need to sit down, Mother?" he asked.

I shook my head. Judah ignored us, attention focused on the doorway. I fanned my face with the edge of my robe. It hardly stirred the air. James pulled the water skin from Judah's belt and offered me a drink. The water revived me.

A ripple moved the crowd, and the boy returned. One of the sons of Jonas followed him. Behind his scruffy beard and tangle of hair, he had kind brown eyes. He introduced himself as Andrew.

"We are Jesus' brothers," Judah said, handing the penny to the boy who bit the metal before pocketing it. His actions made me smile. "We would like to see him."

"Of course, but the Master is teaching now. When the sun goes down, he sends the crowd away. Come back then."

"We have traveled from Nazareth to see him," Judah said, which wasn't completely true. "Can you not see how weary his mother is from the journey?"

They studied me. James tightened his arm around my shoulders. I refused to raise my eyes; instead I studied the fisherman's filthy toes peeking out from beneath his striped robe.

"I will tell him you are here to see him," Andrew said.

It took twice as long for the bulky fisherman to weave through the crowd and back into the building. More time passed. Sweat dripped down my scalp and rolled between my shoulder blades. A persistent itch nagged my forehead where my shawl pressed my hair against the perspiration.

"I do need to sit," I told James the second time he asked.

While he scanned the area for something to use as a seat, another wave parted the sea of bodies. I recognized John, Zebedee and Salome's son, as soon as he left the door of the house.

Before he opened his mouth, I knew what he was going to say. Nothing Judah wanted to hear. I stepped closer to Judah and clenched his forearm, hoping it would stay his temper.

"I apologize, Cousins," John said, "that you've waited so long."

"Is he coming out?"

John shook his head at Judah's question. "The Lord says those who follow his will are his true brethren."

"What?" The expletive that followed shocked me.

Several people nearby turned toward the sudden outburst. Most scowled at Judah, shaking their heads. Many eased further away from us.

"Will you give him a message from us at least?" James, the voice of reason.

"No," Judah said, fisting his hands and shaking his head. "We will speak with him."

"No, you will not, Cousin," John said, pushing out his chest so it bumped against Judah's.

Things were deteriorating rapidly. Two men with such fiery dispositions couldn't disagree without raised voices and physical abuse. I dug my fingernails into Judah's arm. It still took several moments before his glare transferred from Zebedee's youngest son to me.

"Let it go, Judah." I used the same firm tone I had when reprimanding him as a child. "James will give John a message. That is enough."

"It is not enough," Judah said, lowering his face toward me so he could speak more softly. "He owes us common courtesy, at least."

I shook my head. The lining in my throat felt thicker than curds. I doubted I could utter a sound to answer.

My heart understood the sense of betrayal guiding Judah's reactions. In his mind, Jesus had no honor because he shirked the duties of the oldest son. My oldest son. A son whose purpose was so much higher than running a carpentry shop and being the patriarch of our family.

Did I miss spending time with Jesus? Of course. I missed Simon and Rachel, too. It had been much longer than a year since I'd seen either of them.

James wrapped his arm around my shoulders. "Thanks, John," he said to the ruddy youth who looked ready to give Judah a lesson with his fists. "Tell him that Judah has married, and I have opened a shop here in Capernaum."

The red-haired fisherman stepped back, nodding to James. "Of course, Cousin. I will pass along your message."

"Let's go, Judah," James said, an undercurrent of flint in his placating tone. "I want you to see the new shop, Mother. It has a one-room house attached."

I don't remember the trip to his shop, but I did compliment him on the choice.

I am more and more thankful for my middle son. James will be a good husband once he settles down with a wife. Spending time with him dampens the pain this contention between Judah and Jesus causes. I know Judah is hurt, too, and lashes out to hide the heartbreak. I want to tell him I understand, but I fear it would validate his anger.

Jehovah, I am still a mother, but my mothering is finished. How do I guide my adult children? Is it too late for that? Show me the way to be a mother of fully mature men and women.

Lord God, be with Jesus and his disciples. I know you have important work for him to do. I don't want to feel hurt when he doesn't spend time with us. Whatever lies ahead in this traveling ministry, go with him. Protect him, as you did when he was just an infant.

My thanks to you, Yahweh, Lord of Creation.

NAZARETH - SIVAN

MY FORTY-SIXTH YEAR

*I*t was the Sabbath Day. I leaned against the shaded exterior wall of the synagogue, listening to the teaching. Judah's wife, Dafne, shuffled her feet beside me.

Jesus had come home. It was the rumble of his voice drifting to me through the window overhead.

Judah was less than welcoming, so Jesus didn't stay with us. Would Judah ever let the grudge go? Dwelling on the thought filled me with a mixture of sorrow and irritation.

Dafne lightly held my elbow with one hand while adjusting her headdress with the other, her smooth skin barely visible beneath her traditional veil. What would I expect from a rabbi's daughter? At home, she let that formality go.

While her black eyes flitted from face to face, I stared at the unlined skin around them. She seemed so young to me. A lower sweep of my eyes drank in the barely noticeable swell of her abdomen: my first grandchild.

A sudden commotion drew my attention to the door of the synagogue. Shouting?

I pressed closer, dragging Dafne beside me.

"From whence has this man heard these things?"[1xl] one man asked.

"What wisdom is this which is given unto him, that even such mighty works are wrought by his hands?"[2xli]

Pride swelled in my chest. I tried to smother the feeling. It was wrong to accept words of praise toward Jesus as if they were aimed at me. After all, I had nothing to do with his miraculous abilities.

His character surpassed all of us in morality and wisdom. That virtue and integrity wasn't due to my abilities as a mother. A quick look at the squabbling between my other children assured me I failed more often than I succeeded in teaching godliness.

"Is not this the carpenter, the son of Mary?"[3xlii] The angry shout snuffed out the spark of pride.

"The brother of James, and Joses, and of Judah, and Simon?"[4xliii]

"Are not his sisters here with us?"[5xliv]

Things weren't going well. What had Jesus said to make all these men so angry?

"A prophet is not without honor but in his own country." A voice of power: Jesus. "And among his own kin, and in his own house."[6xlv]

Jesus emerged through the doorway. I stepped back, assessing his features. No anger or hurt. Stoic, much like Joseph's had always been. The disciples following him wore expressions of a different nature: anger, frustration, disbelief, and even surprise.

I touched John's arm when he passed me. I wasn't surprised to see his visage red with anger, matching the auburn hair and legendary Zebedee temper.

"Will Jesus come to the house for supper?"

"I will ask, Cousin," he said, but his tone held little hope.

"All of you are welcome, of course."

Beside me, Dafne gasped. My heart shriveled in my chest. I had overstepped again. It seemed impossible that such a child could be the woman of the household, but as Judah's wife, she held that distinction. The twinge of guilt reminded me I was no longer the matriarch. I was little more than a guest in the home I had known for decades.

Dafne's hand covered her mouth, and she shook her head. Of course, she knew that Judah wouldn't be pleased to open his home and share his provisions with Jesus and the hoard of hungry men following him. I tried to apologize with my eyes, while squeezing John's forearm so he wouldn't leave.

"Why is everyone so angry?" Shouldn't the elders have been happy to discuss the Torah with Jesus? They should have wanted him to visit the infirm of the village, at least.

John glared over his shoulder at the doorway of the synagogue. A few men, arms folded across their chests, watched Jesus and his disciples stirring up dust as they tromped down the road.

"They think he's claiming authority that isn't his."

"It is my fault," I whispered.

"Nay. It is the hardness of their own hearts that fuels their animosity."

Tears stung the corners of my eyes. I dabbed them away with the edge of my shawl as I looked into the face of my cousin's son. His passionate glare reminded me of his loyalty to my son.

"I will speak to Jesus," John said, squeezing my hand, "but it appears he is leaving town even now. I must hurry to catch him."

I nodded my thanks as John cast another disparaging glance at the synagogue where more men milled near the doorway, still agitated from the confrontation. Ducking my head, I followed Dafne to the street where Judah's shop and house were located.

Later, Judah fumed and stomped. Dafne had spent several minutes with him after delivering food to the shop at midday. By his demeanor, I assumed she had told him about Jesus. Not that it truly mattered. He and his disciples had departed after the scene in the synagogue.

"Must I remind you, Mother? You are no longer the mistress of this house." Judah sounded like a father scolding a child. How quickly time reverses familial roles.

"Of course." I looked past my son to where Dafne stood, feigning some sort of wiping with a cloth. "I apologize, Dafne. I'll try harder."

My capitulation started an ember of frustration burning deep in my heart. Not only was I unwanted in this household, but they treated me with less respect than a matriarch deserved.

As a widow, my options were few. The oldest son assumed responsibility. Jesus had passed that on to Judah.

"You shouldn't have expected Jesus to take time for us,"

Judah said. "In his eyes, we are no longer even family."

I disagreed but knew arguing would be pointless. After all, he had refused to see us in Capernaum.

It was close to midnight, and I couldn't sleep. Joses skulked in and found me mending clothing by lamplight.

He kissed the top of my head. A whiff of wine and perfume swirled in the air as he moved to sit on the cushion across from me.

"Jesus stopped by," he said.

"I saw him at the synagogue today."

Joses shook his head. "Last night, as Judah and I were closing up the shop, Jesus and one of those fishermen he travels with walked into the workroom."

My fingers stilled against the rough wool. Why had Judah mentioned nothing of this visit? The ball of frustration from earlier awoke like a dog whose tail had been stomped on. A single "Yahweh" in silent prayer stilled it from becoming a full-fledged barking beast.

"Oh?"

"He seemed interested in how the business was going. I showed him the tables for the store in Capernaum. He asked about transport and pricing."

"Your designs improve with each one," I said.

"What would my mother say other than that?" He grinned, relieving the lines around his eyes.

"Did he speak with Judah?"

Joses shrugged, his blunt, calloused fingers drumming against each other.

"Do you feel his anger is justified?"

As the youngest son, Joses bore very few expectations.

We both were powerless, and I wondered if I might find an ally in him.

"Yes, he should feel angry that Jesus dumped all the responsibility on him without even a consultation."

All of this was distant history. If Judah didn't continually fuel his anger, it would have waned by this time.

"However, it left him in a good spot," Joses said, tilting his head against the wall behind him. "I know he grumbled about waiting to marry, but he would have waited longer if he had to establish his own shop, build his own house. He would've had to move to another village, too."

"Have you mentioned this to him?"

Joses looked down at his hands.

"I don't want to get in the middle of things, Mother. I'm the one who has to work with Judah. I don't want him seething in my direction for months on end."

"Months. It has been years." I sighed, hands stilling in the repetitive motion of sewing. "How can he hold a grudge for so long? Especially now that he has everything he wants."

Joses glanced up at me but said nothing. Instead, he moved to the corner of the room where his blankets and woven mat rested in a neat roll against the wall.

It was a hint. I folded my mending project and stood up, steadying myself against the chest where the lamp wobbled at my touch. Lightheadness had become my constant companion and it had grown worse since sleep began evading me most nights.

"Good night, Joses." I spoke toward his back while moving beyond the sheet suspended to form my private sleeping space.

"Good night, Mother."

A wave of longing overcame me as I placed the mending on a small table and sank onto the stool in my room. The bed was narrow, the straw and feather filled mattress dank.

In the dark night, I missed Joseph. He had been gone for fourteen years, and, still, some days the grief stabbed like the first week after his passing. He would have known how to settle the division between his two oldest sons. His calm demeanor and firm words would have stopped Judah's grudge short. How?

I stared at nothing, trying to picture Joseph. His features wavered in my mind, somewhere between the face of James and the hairline and ears of Simon. Memories of him were dusty and difficult to recall. Wondering how he would approach this situation helped nothing. I was not their father; therefore, my words fell on deaf ears. Only for a few short years in their lives did I have influence over them. Those times were long past.

After a few minutes, I heard Joses' movement diminish. I rose from my seat and lifted the mattress from the frame James had constructed for me.

The stack of parchments lay crushed between the goat hide covers I fashioned. I leafed through the stack to a blank sheet, and now I'm nearly finished relating this disheartening day.

Lord Jehovah, I need you to advise me. In the still of this night, I can't hear your voice. Am I no longer useful to you since my mothering years are past? Am I still your handmaiden?

CAPERNAUM - CHESHVAN

MY FORTY-SIXTH YEAR

*W*ithin weeks of the incident in Nazareth, James rented a cart and donkey to carry my meager possessions to Capernaum. As much as I wanted to feel hurt at Judah's rejection, a weight lifted from my chest instead. It was a relief not to face the oppression of Judah's anger and bitterness day after day.

Abigail, on the other hand, had a hard time forgiving Judah for choosing his new wife over me. For weeks after I moved in with James, any mention of Judah's name hardened her jaw into a Roman fortification. Eventually, her heart softened. I hope my continual praise of James aided in the process. Living with him brings moments of pleasure I haven't experienced for a decade.

Someday, Abigail will understand. Two women can't be the matriarch of a single home and family. When the baby comes, I will help her for a few weeks, but my place is with James in the simple room behind his shop.

Watching Abigail blossom with her first child flooded my heart with joy. Now that her time neared, she had confined herself to Reuven's house. Their living arrangements nagged both Abigail and her husband. If not for the child, they might have been ready for a place of their own.

There are always trade-offs, I told her. Would she prefer her own home with no baby on the way? She shook her head.

I've spent more time at the market in recent days. My frequent visits were short and specific. Abigail had the strangest cravings, and her husband's mother had no patience for them. I gladly tromped all over the square, searching to fulfill my daughter's latest penchant.

Today, I went to the marketplace looking for pomegranates. Abigail really just wanted the juice, but I didn't know if any of the merchants sold it. Even after three months in the city, it felt foreign. Nazareth was as familiar to me as a worn sandal, but, with Capernaum's sprawl, I wondered if I would ever feel at home.

At the second fruit vendor's booth, I picked through his assortment of pomegranates while he eyed me like a common thief. Two women in the middle of a conversation stepped up to the stand.

"David's brother traveled over ten miles with his sick son, just to lay him in the streets. Even touching the hem of his garment heals people."

"That can't be true," the second woman said.

"Of course it is. David's nephew's fever left him as soon as the man walked by."

"It makes me wonder if the rumor I've heard is true."

"What rumor?"

I almost smiled at this point. Their conversation reminded me of Sarai. I missed my dear friend and the times we spent rehashing local news.

"I'll take three of those roots and a handful of dried grapes," the first woman said. The second woman placed her own order.

"Apparently, a widow in Nain lost her last living son. He was on the funeral bier, the procession heading toward the grave site."

"Too bad that Jesus of Nazareth hadn't been there to heal him."

Hearing my son's name, I set the fruit down and stared openly at the women.

"That's the thing," the other woman continued, handing coins to the merchant. "He was passing through Nain at that time. He raised the son from the dead."

The first woman gasped, covering her mouth. One of the roots rolled out of her shawl.

"I'm not replacing that," the merchant said.

"Raised him up right off that bier." The woman nodded, opening her own shawl to retrieve her order. They walked away.

I stumbled in the opposite direction, my errand forgotten for a moment. I stopped beside a group of men who paid me no mind but continued their conversation.

"Touched a leper," one man said.

The man beside him shuddered. Leprosy could be spread by a simple touch, which is why lepers had to live in villages away from other people.

"Leper's flesh became smoother than a newborn's."

Men talked about the blind receiving their sight—with a simple touch or sometimes a poultice of clay and spittle. A woman swore some demon-possessed maniac in the region across the sea had been restored into his right mind. Children had been cured from fevers. The lame had been strengthened so they could walk. Jesus healed them all.

"And raised the dead to life," I whispered to myself.

I remembered to purchase two pomegranates for my daughter before stumbling back to her home. When I told her what I had heard about Jesus, she was amazed.

"Do you think it's true?"

I nodded. "Remember the marriage feast in Cana?"

"How is he able to do these miracles?"

"God is with him."

"Who knew my brother would become so famous." She laughed, bringing lightness to the moment.

"Your brother has a special calling from Yahweh." I considered telling her the whole story. Would she think my encounter with a heavenly messenger was a wild tale? Before I could decide, she continued talking, and the moment was lost.

"At least he didn't run off to the wilderness and eat locusts like your cousin."

My cousin? As if John, son of Zacharias, wasn't related to her? I shook my head.

"Some people think locusts are a delicacy," I told her.

She pursed her mouth in distaste and cupped her blossoming midsection.

"You'll make me sick to my stomach, Mother," she said.

My feet felt light when I headed home. Even now, the

aches that usually plague my hips and back at this time of night have been banished. Maybe my body is responding to all the wonderful news of Jesus.

James complimented my dinner, and when I mentioned what I heard in the market, he added a few tidbits of his own about Jesus. Such a different sort of conversation than I ever could have shared with Judah.

At bedtime, James kissed me on the cheek before rolling out his mat near the doorway. He has given up sleeping on the straw-filled mattress. As the master of the house, it should be his, but he won't hear of it. Since moving in with him, my mornings have become nearly pain free.

My children filled me with joy. The oldest was a prophet of God, and my middle son was thoughtful like his father. My sweet, young daughter brought smiles every day I spent with her. Now, praise the Lord, she stood on the cusp of the most rewarding of journeys—motherhood.

JERUSALEM - NISAN

MY FORTY-SEVENTH YEAR

a strange festive air rippled through Jerusalem when we arrived. The buzz seemed centered near the temple, which made sense with the upcoming holy day. I pulled my veil more tightly over my face, attempting to shut out the dust and odors. Nothing dimmed the chaos of animals, vendors, and traffic.

Even though Dafne remained behind in Nazareth, her child due within a few weeks, Judah hoped to lodge with her relatives in the city. James and I accompanied him to the house of Dafne's cousin, a successful scribe. I wished I could be staying with Susanna, but Judah had traveled with us from Capernaum and invited us to lodge with him.

The house's location required traversing the crush of people in the central marketplace. After arriving, my sons and I were escorted to the roof. It wasn't my cousin's house but it provided privacy and a constant breeze to cool me from the heat of travel.

At meal time, the fare was plain and plentiful. I wrapped the vegetables and meat in the bread, rolled it up and savored each filling bite.

"Apparently they're claiming him the son of David now." Even in the noisy room, Judah's raised voice carried to my ears. "A mob sang hosanna as he rode in on a young donkey."

I turned my ears toward the conversation. Our host's reply was lost among the clinking of cups and dishes. Judah's scowl warned they might be discussing Jesus.

"It's not like he asked them to do it." James turned toward his brother with furrowed brows.

"Neither did he forbid them," Judah replied.

Could nothing assuage my second son's anger? He had married and now ran a successful shop, but his bitterness at his older brother wouldn't wane. No matter how many people witnessed the miracles Jesus performed, Judah discounted them. Jesus was nothing but a carpenter, trying to be something special. I shouldn't have been heartbroken at Judah's unbelief. Even the Sanhedrin recognized our cousin John, the baptizer, as a prophet, but Judah ridiculed John's baptism, claiming only priests needed such dousing.

"Some Pharisees ordered him to silence the crowd," our host's apprentice said.

"What was Jesus' response?" James set his rolled bread on the plate in front of him, fixing all his attention on the apprentice. At least one son hungered for the truth.

"If they held their peace, the very stones on the road would cry out."[lxlvi]

Judah shook his head and scoffed. The cousin nodded, thoughtful.

"It almost sounds like scripture," James said.

Yahweh, Lord of Abraham, Isaac and Jacob, I pray both of my sons will accept the truth about Jesus. Soon.

"Nothing from the Torah," Judah said.

"Something from the prophets, perhaps." Dafne's cousin stroked his bearded chin, eyes alight with interest.

Their conversation turned to a debate about the reliability of the texts from the prophets of old.

I stopped listening. Jesus was here. I wanted to see him, but if crowds continued to flock to him, I wouldn't be able to get close enough.

THE NEXT DAY, I sat mending some clothes for our hostess. James burst into the room, panting, dirt streaking his cheeks, and demanded to see Judah.

Laying aside my cloth and needle, I followed him into the courtyard. Judah reclined in shade provided by a blanket suspended on two poles. By his crossed arms, I could tell he still pouted because we hadn't wanted to leave today. Why fight the multitude now that Pesach was finished? What was one more day?

"Come with me, brother," James said.

"What is it?"

"Jesus."

Judah swatted at his brother like a pesky fly.

I couldn't remain in the background. "What of Jesus?" My heart leapt into my throat.

The solemn expression James wore proclaimed more than

a hundred words. I covered my mouth with my hand. Why did my fingers tremble so?

James wrapped me in his strong embrace, always so much more demonstrative than Joseph or Judah. I tried to breathe against the tightness in my chest.

Rumors had circulated that the Council had marked Jesus as an extremist and heretic. Only his popularity with the multitudes kept him safe from their clutches.

"Pilate is bringing out two prisoners."

Prisoners? Why would Pilate have anything to do with the Council?

"Common practice during the feast," the cousin said, entering with a wineskin and several goblets. "It's a political ploy, trying to garner favor from the natives."

"What do you mean?" Judah asked, taking a cup of drink from the host.

"Oh, he always has some Israelites imprisoned but he lets the crowd free one of them. A show of mercy or some such."

"Jesus?" I couldn't form a complete thought.

The cousin glanced at me before sliding onto the couch Judah had vacated when James roused him.

"Apparently, he was arrested last night," James said.

I couldn't contain the gasp. I clapped my hand over my mouth to keep any others from escaping. Judah narrowed his eyes and drank from his cup.

"I'm sorry, Mother, but I can't say I'm surprised," Judah said. "You shouldn't be either. His teachings contradict tradition. He has no formal training so he won't be accepted by the Sanhedrin. As for a proper background—"

Proper background? Emotion choked me, but I could

never have explained how their brother's background was beyond proper for the highest position in the land. The Council cared too much about power and too little about truth.

"I want you to go to the Judgment Hall with me," James pleaded with voice and eyes.

Judah shook his head, dropping his eyes rather than meeting his brother's gaze.

"I'll go," I said.

James shook his head. "No, Mother. I wouldn't feel comfortable taking you there."

"Usually draws an unruly mob," the cousin said. "Everyone wants to shout and scream, pretend they're part of something."

"I knew we should have left this morning," Judah grumbled.

Sudden fury dwarfed my fear. I was finished with this jealousy and contention. I stomped over to my second son and pulled his chin up, as if he were a small child.

His hand reached to push me away but froze when his eyes met mine. What was it he saw in my face that stopped him?

"Enough. Jesus gave up everything, and you inherited it." If no one else wanted to confront him with the truth, I would. "Most second sons would rejoice to have such security. All you can do is complain and condemn."

James sidled close to me, ready to intervene. Did he really think his brother would harm me? Violence had never been part of their upbringing. Joseph hardly raised his voice in anger. Perhaps more use of the rod would have kept Judah from his unbecoming attitude.

"Go with your brother," I said.

Judah opened and closed his mouth several times. I turned away from him, striding back into the house, aware of the hitch in my hip with every step. At the last moment, I turned, scorching Judah with a look before meeting James' calm gaze.

"Bring me word."

Thus began the longest hours of my life. Longer even than laboring to bring Jesus into the world. Longer than plodding through the dust to Bethlehem or Egypt. Almost unendurably long.

Lord God, where are you?

THE MOB in front of Pilate's hall stretched into the surrounding streets. It wasn't a quiet or docile group waiting for Pilate's pronouncement. James and Judah couldn't get close enough to see too much detail, but the city was abuzz with the story.

This is how they relayed their brother's trial to me.

Pilate brought Jesus onto the porch of the great stone edifice. The accusers, chief priests and scribes, stood at the base of the steps. Behind them, the mob pressed, wanting to see what prisoner the governor would release as an act of good faith.

"Ye have brought this man unto me, as one that perverteth the people: and, behold, I, having examined him before you, have found no fault in this man touching those things whereof ye accuse him."[2][xlvii]

This caused a stir among the council members. The crowd picked up on their anxiety. Murmurs flowed like water. "What are they saying?"

"No, nor yet Herod, for I sent you to him; and, lo, nothing worthy of death is done unto him."[3][xlviii]

"He deserves death according to our laws," said the chief priest. A murmur of assent rose from the council.

A heartbeat later, the multitude echoed that agreement.

"I will therefore chastise him, and release him."[4][xlix] Pilate turned away from them.

Another prisoner stumbled forth, pushed by a Roman centurion. The other man was a murderer and insurrectionist who had caused much upheaval in the surrounding country before coming to Jerusalem and being arrested. It was clear, Pilate wanted the crowd to choose one of these two men for release.

"Away with this man Jesus," the crowd cried. "Release unto us Barabbas."[51]

I still can't comprehend their demand. Barabbas was a murderer. Jesus was a miracle-working teacher. The crowd's request made no sense.

"Will ye that I release unto you the King of the Jews?" Pilate asked, pointing toward Jesus.

King of the Jews was the accusation the council brought against him, saying he claimed to be a king but Caesar was their king.

Starting small, the chant of "Barabbas" floated in the

square. It gained momentum, as, from front to back, the mob chanted the murderer's name.

"What shall I do then with Jesus which is called Christ?"[6li]

A roar greeted this inquiry: "Crucify him."

Pilate couldn't be heard by any but those at the front, when he asked, "Why? What evil hath he done?"[7lii]

The chanting grew to a fevered pitch. "Crucify him. Crucify him."

I couldn't hold back the tears as James recounted the tale to me. And those spots here try to ruin the ink of my words.

Wasn't this the same crowd that had sang hosanna to him yesterday? Didn't they claim him to be their long-awaited king? And now they would see him die at the hand of Roman executioners?

I couldn't bear to witness this horror. Thinking of it crushed my heart. Drawing breath became excruciating. Words from long ago pushed at the back of my mind. Simeon had claimed a sword would pierce my soul. All the other moments I thought the prophecy was coming true paled beside this one. My heart and soul bled from the wound caused by this sudden violence against my promised son.

"When?" Somehow I asked my sons this simple question.

"Mother, you should return to Nazareth with me," Judah said, no anger in his tone.

I knew he grieved at this turn of events. Whatever bitterness his heart held against his brother, it wasn't enough to wish this evil upon him.

"James, when will they crucify your brother?"

"Tomorrow morning, Mother." James choked on the words.

I squeezed his strong, calloused carpenter's hand between mine. Hands so like his father's. How could the memory of Joseph's hands seem so clear when his face was little more than a shadow? How I wished he were here now. He would know how to comfort me. How to help Jesus.

"I am not returning to Nazareth with you, Judah."

He shook his head. I didn't expect him to abandon me, but I knew that neither of them would permit me to do that which I wanted tomorrow.

"I am going to Susanna's," I announced.

Both of my sons seemed slightly relieved.

"I will take you, Mother," James said.

I thanked him and gathered my things. I would never return to this abode. How could I look on it and not think of these bitter tidings?

Somehow, I held myself together until I was in my cousin's guest chamber. After that, I'm not sure how I even saw the parchment to scribble this entry.

Yahweh, why is this evil happening to your son, the Promised One of Israel? I don't understand.

How can I bear this?

I cannot.

JERUSALEM - NISAN

MY FORTY-SEVENTH YEAR

*A*ir stagnated around the press of people. It was not even the third hour of the day, and a multitude lined the streets. Beneath my feet, the ground trembled at the cadence of soldiers parading. No jangling of armor could be heard above the angry shouts of the post-feast worshipers. Many stayed in Jerusalem because of the High Sabbath on the morrow followed by a single preparation day and the true Sabbath. Even though I had never seen Jerusalem streets without throngs of temple-bound countrymen, I had never seen such riotous behaviors from these supposed devotees of Yahweh.

Susanna pressed her arm around mine as the tumult of bodies jarred me, attempting to separate us. My sister Mary stood at my back, and her hand brushed my arm as the crowd writhed. Somewhere nearby, John, who had accompanied us onto the streets, watched over us. But who could find anyone amidst such an oppressive host? Most of the other disciples of

Jesus, including Mary's son James, who was one of the twelve Jesus had named apostles, hid beneath cloaks. Their fear sickened me even while I understood its source.

If Messiah could not stand against Rome, what could a handful of common men do?

As the lead soldiers passed into view, Mary Magdalene pushed her way to the front of a group of women. All of them covered their heads with mourning shawls and wailed as if they were in a funeral procession. Mary's face flushed from her effort but remained smooth with incomprehensible peace. Tears streaked down her cheeks, reminding me to brush the moisture off my own face. My hands were already muddy from the combination of dust and tears.

The forward progress of the soldiers halted. A command from the center divided the squad of armed men into a retaining wall, holding back the mass of people anxious to see the criminals marching to execution. How had I ended up in this place?

One of the prisoners had fallen beneath the crossbeams of the Roman torture device. On the opposite side of the road, a soldier jerked a man away from his family. His face was darker than a native Israelite's. His shoulders bunched beneath a handwoven tunic of dark blue. Even with his head bowed, the man stood as tall as the soldier pulling him toward the pile of bloody rags crushed beneath the massive cross.

"An islander," Susanna whispered in my ear.

"Cyrenian," said my sister.

With a mighty grunt, the Cyrenian heaved the cross onto his own shoulder. His knees buckled for a moment as he resettled the weight on his broad back. He stepped into line at the front of the procession. Three soldiers approached the bloody figure; one kicked it as the other two jerked it upright.

It was a man. Or what was left of a man. Roman crucifixion started with a lashing that left most criminals flayed. Dehydration killed them if the blood loss didn't do the job first.

The beaten form was bumped between the two soldiers until he seemed to find balance. He stumbled forward, steadying himself on the unfinished beams that had previously crushed him.

Cries rose from the crowd. "Deceiver" or "master" and sometimes even "rabbi." Was that Jesus? I couldn't identify the abused form as my son.

He passed in front of where I stood. Only a thin line of heated bodies separated me from my firstborn, and still I did not recognize him. I pressed my hand more tightly over my mouth and nose, fighting a sudden urge to vomit.

Tingles of terror prickled my skin when a unified wail rose from the company of women. Mary Magdalene thrust beyond the wall of soldiers, prostrating herself beside Jesus' feet. The centurion grabbed her by the shoulders and threw her back into the crowd of shrieking women, with little more effort than a boy tossing a pebble.

Jesus turned his face toward the lamenting women. Beneath the spiky thorns, I could make out one of his eyes, calm and clear in his mangled face. Puffy red skin swelled where the other eye should have been.

"Daughters of Jerusalem," he cried, his voice carrying above the moans of the women and the threats of the crowd, "weep not for me, but weep for yourselves, and for your children."[1liii]

His words brought a new gush of moisture to my eyes. Keening rose in my throat, blocking out the remainder of his words. Through the blur of tears, I saw the centurion prod my son with a spear, nearly toppling him again, until he followed the parading soldiers.

Once the prisoners and their escorts emerged from the city gates, most of the crowd faded back inside the walls. The waiting crowd of witnesses lining the road to the skull-shaped hill took up their chants and mocking. My sister pressed into my side while Susanna tightly held my other arm. Our scraggly cluster hobbled behind the marching soldiers.

A man from the crowd pushed toward us, leering and spewing spittle with the obscenities he screamed in my face. In an instant, John stood in front of us, shoving the man, older than him but slighter, out of our way.

Onward we marched, ascending the craggy hillock. Strange buzzing filled my ears, drowning out the shouts of the multitude. Beneath my feet, the ground seemed to lurch. Everything blurred.

I don't remember reaching the pinnacle, but somehow, I stood at the base of the crosses. Three men hung from the scarred wooden boards, pinioned by nails driven into their hands and feet. Naked skin exposed to the elements would speed the process of death.

Hours of agony lay ahead for these criminals—and my innocent son. Jesus, who the messenger of Jehovah had promised would reign over the house of Jacob forever.

Simeon's promised sword plunged deeper into my heart,

wounding the deepest part of me. The place where I'd pondered the secrets of the messenger's words from three decades ago and the thrill of the shepherds. I bled as profusely as my precious Jesus.

"He saved others, let him save himself,"[2][liv] a group of scribes called, pointing at Jesus.

Others chided, "If thou be the Christ, the chosen of God, come down."[3][lv] These men were garbed in the robes of rulers but screeched like common publicans.

Jesus said, "Father, forgive them,"[4][lvi] but the rest of his words drowned beneath the jeers of the rabble surrounding us.

They mocked the writing on the sign above his head: [5][lvii]

"If thou be the King of the Jews, save thyself."[6][lviii]

As the sun rose higher in the sky, many of the onlookers turned back toward the city. They were no longer entertained by the awful display of inhumanity. Their desertion cleared the way for our knot of mostly women to press closer to the crosses. A ring of soldiers separated us from those suffering their executions.

"Woman,"[7][lix] Jesus called.

I shaded my eyes from the glaring sun with my shawl and looked upward. His voice sounded garbled, coming from the mangled face I hardly recognized.

"Behold thy son."[8][lx]

How could I look away? The prophecy of Simeon was fulfilled. A sword pierced my soul, and the rending stopped my lungs from drawing air. John steadied me, laying his strong hand on my shoulder.

"Behold thy mother!"[9][lxi]

John stepped into the space behind me, pressing against my trembling back. "Mother," he whispered in my ear.

If only Judah had been here to see this gesture. In the clutches of an agonizing death, Jesus—the brother he despised for walking away from familial duties—addressed them and freed Judah from his responsibility to me. John's rapid acceptance of such a duty, though he was much younger than most of the disciples and yet unmarried, shamed me. Why did my own son find me too much of a burden?

Shadows crept over the gathering, as if clouds covered the sun. The sky remained clear, however, but the golden globe darkened. Soldiers hurried to light torches, setting them around the perimeter of the hill.

"What does this mean? It is only the sixth hour,"[10][lxii] I heard a soldier ask the centurion.

My lungs remembered to breathe. I gasped and wilted against John. One of his arms encircled my waist while the other pressed beneath my shoulder. I was thankful for the darkness. It matched the barrenness in my heart and soul. How could a heart as crushed as mine continue to beat?

"I thirst,"[11][lxiii] Jesus called out, his cry echoed by the other men on their crosses.

Three soldiers stepped forward to thrust liquid-drenched hyssop toward the faces of the dying men. My own throat ached, constricted by emotion. How much worse it must be for Jesus. Again, I thanked the Lord that I could not distinguish much in the flickering torch light.

The crowd thinned further as the darkness wore on. Jesus cried out two more times, startling me from my trance-like state. Each utterance shattered my heart further. It would never be whole again.

"It is finished,"[121][lxiv] he finally bellowed.

Will it ever be finished? If the pain doesn't diminish over time, I will surely die from it.

John's arms tightened around my shoulders. "Come, Mother," he said. "Let's go home."

"But his body . . ." My lips trembled so much I didn't know if the words made sense.

John nodded toward two well-dressed men standing close to the centurion. "Those disciples will see to it, Mother."

Disciples? They looked like members of the Sanhedrin or possibly spiteful Pharisees.

Numbness in my extremities made resisting impossible, so I let him lead me along. I tripped down the deserted hill-side, my arm securely cradled in his.

Finally, the shadow of the gate announced our arrival into the city. The streets were nearly deserted, as if the dark after-noon was actually midnight.

Bleakness sucked the energy from my limbs. I just wanted to sleep. Perhaps I would awaken and discover it all had been a terrible dream.

No. Not a dream. A nightmare.

DARK DAYS - NISAN

MY FORTY-SEVENTH YEAR

"Joseph of Arimathea convinced Pilate to release the body to him," John told me. His reddened eyes informed me that he hadn't slept much.

I stared at his blunt fingers, relishing the feel of the calloused fingertips stroking the back of my hand. So like Father's strong hands. Memories of more pleasant times cavorted through my mind, trying to keep the horror of the past days in check.

"The tomb is in the garden near the execution site."

Other details flowed as Mary asked him a question. I glanced idly at the sealed jars of salve on the table. How could my eldest son be buried without proper anointing? One more travesty of justice. A small one, compared to the slaughter of an innocent man.

Slaughter of an innocent.

Flashes of the sacrifice of the Pesach lamb flooded my mind. That death was what the Holy Father God demanded in payment for sins. I pictured my father laying his work-scarred hands on the head of the fuzzy lamb, heard the priest petition God to accept this substitutionary sacrifice, and watched the knife slash across the white wool. Blood drained into a bowl.

Conversation flowed around me. Susanna laid measuring instruments and mixing utensils beside the frankincense and spices. Salome patted John's shoulder as she passed with bunches of dried herbs in hand.

The picture of the lamb pushed its way into the scene on Golgotha yesterday. More innocent blood flowed from the pale skin of my son. The two scenes blended. The juxtaposition meant something important. My flummoxed brain whirred, trying to make sense of the overlapping pictures.

"Mother, would you like to lie down?"

John's tender voice pierced the fog around my mind. I turned to stare into his hazel eyes. My fingers pushed a lock of his thick auburn hair off his forehead. Coarse, like a goat hide before I cured it.

"The Pesach sacrifice," I said. "An innocent slain for our sins."

My mouth felt dry. John handed me a goblet. Warm water splashed across my tongue and soothed my tight throat.

"Jesus was innocent," I said, my fingers trembling as I held the empty goblet toward him.

John took the goblet away. My hand trembled beneath the squeeze of his fingers. His eyes were warm, but he said nothing.

An urgency pushed against me. "He had to die."

Tears flooded my eyes. No wonder I felt as parched as the

earth in summertime. Every little thing caused grief to seep from behind my eyelids.

"Come, Mother," he said, guiding me away from the table.

The other women, clucking or patting my back, watched me leave the room where the preparation of burial salves would take place. As the mother of the deceased, I should pray and sing while mixing the ingredients in proper proportion. I wanted to do those things for my son, but I couldn't find the strength to resist the insistent pressure from John's strong hands.

I hobbled through the doorway and melted onto the bed.

"It's important," I whispered.

John fluffed a pillow beneath my head. I curled my knees against my chest, hugging them to still the incessant trembling. John drew a linen sheet over my body.

Nothing covered the gaping hole in the center of my being. Memories and emotions bled out. Could I die from such a wound? *A sword shall pierce through thy own soul also.*

I clenched John's hand. "Remember what Zacharias' son said of him?"

John knelt on the floor beside my pallet, his scruffy features even with my face.

"You should rest," he said.

"John, do you remember? James repeated it to me. It threw Judah into a fit."

John's full eyebrows drew together. Would he remember? Would he agree with my conclusion? One that made the senseless death have eternal significance?

It wasn't senseless. *Substitutionary.* Like the Pesach lamb.

"Do you mean when he called him the Lamb of God?"

I nodded. The mourning shawl, draped over my hair, snagged against the pillow. My head barely moved, hindered by the outward trappings of my inward struggle.

"You're right, Mother. It is important." His lips brushed my forehead, a gentle touch, a father's touch. "You rest. I will think on it."

His smile almost reached his eyes. A furrow appeared between his ruddy brows.

My eyes fluttered. On the back of my closed eyelids, the two scenes slid together again. Father slitting the throat of the Pesach sacrifice. Blood dripping from the flayed flesh of my innocent son.

No, I thought, as my mind drifted away on the rising tide of grief. The Son of the Highest, the angel told me. The Lamb of God, who takes away the sins of the world.[lxv]

A salve for my broken heart had been found.

AFTER ANOTHER LONG night of weeping, the Sabbath passed. On the eastern horizon, a line of golden orange announced the coming sunrise. The streets, well-marked by smoldering torches, seemed barren. Only a few merchants moved in the doorways of shops. A fire kindling in the stone oven beside a bakery lent a smoky fragrance to the predawn stillness.

Following the path to the garden, I trudged beside my sister.

"Will the guards allow us in?" Salome's question

reminded me of the report her older son, James, brought to us the previous day.

A contingent of Roman soldiers guarded the tomb of Joseph of Arimathea. Pilate had set his own seal on the rock covering the burial chamber from exposure.

"At least we can ask them to remove the stone," Mary Magdalene said.

"If they allow it." My sister Mary squeezed my elbow.

"We could never budge the behemoth on our own," Salome said, attempting to smile.

My own lips couldn't respond. A foreign hope burned in my chest. I fostered it by mentally repeating every phrase the messenger said when he announced my pregnancy. The joyful proclamations of the shepherds from that night some thirty-three years before added fodder. Recalling the wise astrologers who visited us before the flight to Egypt stacked another twig on this sputtering flame.

Birdsong burst from a bush on my left. I stared into the foliage, searching for the musician. Fluttering from higher branches drew my attention. Another bird chirruped, and, on the opposite side of the path, a third bird added his voice.

Ahead of me, Mary Magdalene gasped and bolted forward. Susanna and Mary froze in their tracks beside me. Salome stumbled against us at our sudden stop.

An enormous stone lay on the ground exposing a crypt to the early morning light. My heart leapt in my chest, its pounding drowned out the sounds of waking birds.

Mary disappeared into the tomb. I followed, several steps behind.

On the ledge inside, the burial clothes seemed

untouched. My gaze drifted toward the head of the tightly wrapped bundle. The napkin covering the face was not on the shelf. More surprising, no face could be seen within the wrappings. It was nothing but an empty shell!

Energy surged through my limbs. Even as my mind whirled at the impossibility of the sight, my heart soared.

Two men suddenly appeared. My companions and I gasped and stumbled backward. My shoulders pressed into the side of the cave. One man stood beside the feet of the empty grave clothes while the other stood at the head.

"Why seek ye the living among the dead?"[2][lxvi] one of the men asked.

Mary squeezed my hand in hers. Her fingers trembled against mine. A quick glance to either side proved that the others stood dumbfounded, aghast at the sudden appearance of the men.

I shook my head. Not men, messengers from God, much like the one who had visited me so many years ago.

"He is not here, but is risen." [3][lxvii]The angel beside the head of the wrappings gestured toward the empty shell in the alcove. "Remember how he spake unto you when he was yet in Galilee, saying, 'The Son of Man must be delivered into the hands of sinful men, and be crucified and the third day rise again.'"[4][lxviii]

The other three nodded their heads. I couldn't do the same. Judah had forbade me from joining the cluster of women who traveled with Jesus, caring for his daily need of food. What the messengers said, however, sparked the memory of my companions.

"Go your way," the other messenger said, "tell his disciples and Peter that he goeth before you into Galilee: there shall ye see him, as he said unto you."[5][lxix]

Joy flooded inside me. I pressed behind Salome as she exited the confines of the tomb. Death was not the end for the Son of God.

My sandals scuffled on the slanting path. As Mary joined me, we ran back toward the city.

Wind kissed my cheeks and whistled alongside my ears. I gasped for breath, and our pace slowed. I hadn't run so far since I left Father's farm. My heart pounded in my chest. I glanced at the flushed faces of my sister and cousins. My lips wobbled into a smile.

"Is it true then?" my sister asked.

"Those were messengers from Jehovah," I said. "I've seen one before."

Mary nodded. She had heard the story. Now, perhaps she believed it.

"We must tell the disciples." Salome fanned her flushed features with the ends of her shawl.

I turned to look behind us. We stood where the path merged into the road leading through the city gates.

"Where is Mary?"

The others turned to gaze up the path we had descended so hurriedly.

"Should we wait for her?" my sister asked.

We huddled together, whispering furiously to each other.

Mary Magdalene descended several minutes later, jogging down the hill. A smile wreathed her tear-streaked face and made her glow as brightly as the sun which rose behind her.

"He's alive," she gasped. "I saw him. I spoke with him."

We gaped at her. A spike of jealousy twisted behind my breastbone. Why had he chosen to appear to this woman rather than to me? I recognized the emotion as a snare of the tempter and brushed the thought away. Had I faithfully followed him? This woman had dedicated her life to him for nearly three years.

"Will you tell Peter and the others?" I asked.

She nodded and sprinted toward the city. If only my legs and lungs could have endured it, I would have run through the city shouting the news.

He's alive. My son lives.

GALILEE - NISAN

MY FORTY-SEVENTH YEAR

*T*he road north was dusty and long. The disciples who had been so close to Jesus the last several years wandered back to Capernaum and the homes of Peter, Andrew and James bar-Zebedee. John stayed beside me, demanding the shuffling group stop to rest when my hip ached and I limped too much.

I had insisted on traveling with John. I told him it was so I could choose what items to bring from James' small house, but that was only half the reason. The messengers at the tomb said that Jesus would see us in Galilee. I wanted to see my son. My head knew he lived again, after all he was the Promised One, but my heart still ached from the ugly crucifixion and the days of weeping that followed it.

John left me at James' shop, promising to return before evening. James hugged me and apologized profusely for abandoning me in Jerusalem. Eventually, he returned to work, even leaving me alone to retrieve wood from a supplier.

I rolled my extra tunic and robe into the woven blanket from Elisabeth. She'd sent it only a few months before she passed, and it had adorned my marriage bed from that day forward. Parts of the edges frayed, but those places were nearly silken from constant handling.

Yahweh, I don't know what lies ahead of me. I'm not eager to stay in Jerusalem or in Zebedee's house in Bethsaida, but I trust that John is exactly who you want caring for me. Jesus...

The sob rose suddenly. Its quality was wistful instead of anguished. Would Jehovah grant my greatest desire? It seemed selfish to pray for it when He'd given me so much already.

I'd had years with Messiah. I'd held his hand through childhood prayers. His voice had read scripture from our family copy of Isaiah's prophecies. His small hands had soothed the agony of three childbirths, not completely alleviating them, but with a special healing he later used on the multitudes.

I remembered his young voice apologizing as I labored with Joses. He wasn't supposed to use his touch that way now that he had a better understanding.

"It's fine, son." I squeezed his fingers during the next contraction, but the soothing relief didn't come. I'd strained through the pain to deliver my firstborn, and I would do the same with my fifth-born son and my second-born daughter.

I blinked back to the present. After straightening the pallet on the lovely frame James made, I turned toward the main living area. A shadow shifted across the doorway.

Jesus. He held out his hand. His hazel eyes fixed on mine,

somehow different than I remembered. Everything about him seemed softer, more perfect. How could this be?

"*Ima*," he said. He hadn't called me the nickname for decades.

Tears burned my eyes. I shuffled forward, hesitating for a moment at the unfamiliarity of his features. His lips quirked as he opened his arms.

I threw myself against his chest. "You're here."

Warm hands patted my shoulder. His body felt strange beneath my embrace, sturdy but insubstantial. It made no sense.

"I must speak with James."

"He went for supplies."

Jesus nodded. Our gazes met and held. Something powerful welled inside him. My knees trembled.

I backed away and knelt before him. "Messiah, my Lord."

"You've always believed in me." A quiet timber reminiscent of Heli entered his tone. Part of my father lived on in this God-man, just like it did in his brother James.

"I didn't understand—"

Fingers touched my hair, uncovered in the warmth of the house while I was sorting my few belongings.

"Your understanding is still incomplete. That is the way of things."

My son, always wise beyond his years. Or maybe those were the moments his Godhood shined through his speech.

"I mourned your death. If I had truly known—"

He lifted me to my feet. It was a strange sensation because I didn't feel hands on me so much as a pressure. When I stood before him, he settled a finger on my jaw.

I recalled the baby he'd been long ago doing the same thing. As if our skin touching imparted a special emotion to him. Now, as he gazed beyond my eyes into the scarred soul bearing the promised sword-wound, the touch granted a flow of supernatural peace. The kind I found after heartfelt prayer that melded with contentment while I worshipped Yahweh in the court of women.

A gasp slipped from my parted lips.

"Share everything with John, mother. He needs you more than you need him."

Of course, Jesus had chosen John for a reason. After all, I had four other sons who could have cared for me.

"James has important work. He won't have the means to listen like John will."

I nodded, but I didn't understand. Not really.

"Your brother believes now."

Jesus ducked his chin. A small, somewhat sad smile tilted his mouth.

"They all will."

Even Judah?

I didn't voice the question. I know I didn't.

"Especially Judah. But he will feel more guilt than the others."

As he should. He'd been unrelenting in his harshness toward Jesus, while the others let him go his way.

One look into my son's eyes and I knew these condemning thoughts toward Judah were not right. Hadn't Yahweh forgiven my harshness? Judah deserved the same mercy.

"Forgive me." A sharp pain lanced through my chest and then faded.

"Always. Forgiveness is what my life is about."

And his death. I heard the unspoken addition.

Before I could return his gentle touch, he slipped through the doorway. I heard James' startled greeting.

My sons would finally understand everything I had spent a lifetime trying to comprehend. And my life wasn't finished. There was always more to learn.

Yahweh, deepen my understanding.

24

JERUSALEM - IYAR

MY FORTY-SEVENTH YEAR

*T*oday was goodbye, and I didn't get to say it to his face. My firstborn son has gone to his father's house, never to be seen by these eyes again.

It was nearing evening when we gathered in the room of Mary Mark's home. Simon Peter led the gathering.

Seated on my right was Judah, and on my left, James. After all of the miracles and teachings of their oldest brother, only seeing him resurrected from the dead compelled them to believe. Joses leaned against the wall beside his cousin James, anxious to hear Jesus' final words. Across the room, John bar Zebedee caught my eye and nodded. I returned the gesture. James pulled me closer to his side, acknowledging my new guardian with a dip of his bearded chin.

"Are you sure, Mother?" His breath tickled my ear.

I nodded. After all, Jesus instructed John to see after me. It was his dying wish.

Except he wasn't dead. My heart danced strange rhythms

when I considered his appearances over the past several weeks. What mother can say she suffered the pain of watching her son die and the joy of beholding him restored to life?

Lord God of Abraham, you bless me beyond what my feeble humanity deserves.

Jehovah is mighty and has done to me great things.[1lxx]

Holy is his name.

His mercy is on them that fear him from generation to generation.[2lxxi]

He had showed strength with his arm[3lxxii]. (Who else defeated death?)

He hath scattered the proud in the imagination of their hearts.[4lxxiii]

He hath put down the mighty from their seats, and exalted them of low degree[5lxxiv] (who could be lower than me?).

He hath filled the hungry with good things; and the rich he hath sent empty away.[6lxxv]

These words, spoken after Elisabeth blessed me three and thirty years ago, rang like a melody through my mind. Echoing in my heart, the praise expanded until a shout of joy pressed against my throat.

"We are to wait for the promise of the baptism of the Holy Ghost." Peter's words drew me back into the moment.

After the clouds had captured the Savior out of view, the eleven apostles stared into the sky. Perhaps, they would stand there still if two men in white hadn't startled them from their reverie. These sounded like the same messengers who greeted us by the tomb. Was it just forty days ago?

The path ahead involved sharing the good news that the Messiah had come. The ultimate sacrifice had been made. Eternal redemption from sin's penalty had been paid in full. No more yearly treks into the holiest place by the high priest are required. God's Lamb had died and our sins have been covered by His precious blood.

James squeezed my hand. Hot drops splashed on our joined palms. I've been crying. I hadn't realized it. Shouldn't all my tears be spent?

Today is marked with the same spirit of change I experienced long ago when the messenger told me about Jesus' unique conception. I had no idea the grief, tumult, and joy that would follow his pronouncement. How could I? I knew so little then. Now, I have borne seven children, buried a husband and a son. Have these experiences prepared me for the unknown path ahead?

For three years, many in this room have been caught up in the fervor of the Messiah's teaching and miracles. After prompting him to provide wine at the marriage feast in Cana, I followed his deeds through secondhand accounts. So much that was shrouded in mystery became clear after his resurrection.

I finally understood his destiny. "My kingdom is not of this world,"[7][lxxvi] Jesus said.

And yet, I know Jesus reigns, as the angel Gabriel promised me so long ago.

The difference is hope.

We expected a conquering king, and Yahweh sent a humble servant. Our hearts exalt Messiah onto the throne of his father David. Jehovah exalts him higher, above the earth and even surpassing the heavens. Traditions taught us to look for a peace-bringer, the Prince of Peace. Only it wasn't an external peace in His hands but a deep abiding internal quietness.

James' hand slid away. The movement caught his brother's attention. My eyes locked with Judah's, the son who is now the patriarch of my family. Hollowness filled his eyes, and I saw the self-condemnation there.

I threaded my hand through the crook of his arm and patted the exposed skin. One son is gone forever, but this stubborn son of mine is real and present. He whose grief is weighted with guilt.

"He forgave," I whispered.

Judah tilted his head closer, and I repeated the words, my lips nearly brushing his ear. Even after days away from it, the scent of wood clung to his skin. The smell of home.

His eyes met mine, and I nodded.

"You can't know that." He leaned his forehead against the side of my hair. Even through the shawl, I felt the wetness of his shame.

"He said it." My voice was firm. "On the cross just before he died. He said, 'Father, forgive them; for they know not what they do.' [8lxxvii]That means you, Judah."

He pulled away, rubbing the back of his hand across his cheeks. Did he think I hadn't seen his tears? His eyes widened with shifting emotions. Doubt, shame, hope, disbelief.

A lull in Peter's speech drew my attention to the front of the room. When I looked at Judah again, firm confidence replaced the uncertainty. His jaw was set. His disbelief had fervor, and I expected his acceptance would burn just as brightly.

For a moment, I held them all close in my heart—my children: Jesus, Judah, James, Simon, Rachel, Joses, and Abigail.

Thank you, Yahweh, for each moment I've had with them.

Jesus may be absent from the daily dance of our lives, but the flame of his love burns brightly. More brightly even than the star which heralded his birth to those visitors from the East.

One son is gone, but the beating in my chest assures me of his presence. Separation means nothing now.

A mother's heart always cherishes.

A mother's heart never forgets.

PERSONAL REFLECTIONS

Every author's dream: reader reads book and cannot put it down. Afterward, reader tells everyone they know about the book and write reviews for it on Amazon, Goodreads and every other major book seller's site. Reader misses the characters so reads the book again, more slowly.

Of course, I hope that has been your experience with *Reflections from a Pondering Heart*. But more than that, I pray that God has used my story to open your eyes to the characters **behind** the Bible stories we love.

In keeping with my hope and prayer, I've designed this section of the book to help you reflect on specific aspects of the story. Perhaps you read the book before realizing this section was available; that's fine. However, to get the most out of these reflective questions and thoughts, refer to them at the end of every chapter (or several chapters in a few cases).

Before you begin: How do you imagine Mary (before reading this fictionalization)?

Chapter One

What age did you imagine Mary was when the angel spoke with her?

Did the idea that she was thirteen years old offend you? Put you off? Why or why not?

*This is a cultural norm for those in Middle Eastern societies but seems wrong to those of us raised in Western cultures. Regardless of what you think, remember that to Mary, getting married at the age of thirteen to a much older man would be expected, the course most young women took.

Read Luke 1:28-38. What part of the angel's message do you think amazed Mary the most? Excited her?

Imagine an angel appeared and gave you this message. How would you react?

Mary refers to herself as "the handmaid of the Lord." Why do you think she did this? What does that title mean to you?

Describe Heli and Mary's relationship.

Her stepmother, Anna, is very disapproving. Why might this be?

If this situation (pregnant before marriage by the Holy Ghost) happened to you, would your father be as accepting as Heli? Why or why not?

Heli chooses to send Mary away. This was also a common practice in American culture until the 1970s. What do you think prompted his actions?

Chapter Two

Mary gets to walk for several days after hearing her unbelievable news. Do you tend to worry or pray when you're walking?

Does walking help you work out your problems?

Elisabeth is old and pregnant. What sort of things might she be feeling?

Describe Mary's relationship with Elisabeth.

*The Bible doesn't say much more than that they were cousins. In order to rationalize why Heli would send Mary so far away, I created a scenario that made Elisabeth more like a surrogate mother to Mary. Fact: many women died in childbirth during the first century. A relative would likely have been the one to come and care for Heli and his orphans. A spinster, or childless, woman would be one without her own familial responsibilities and thus available to become the nanny for a short time.

Read Luke 1:41-56. (Mary's part in this conversation is used at the very end of the book.) What other things do you imagine these two pregnant women discussed during their three-month visit?

Chapters Three through Five

At first, Joseph doesn't believe Heli's tale. What would it take for a man to believe an angel had impregnated his future wife?

How would the cultural norms we face change this situation?

*Regardless of personal our convictions, the fact is clear that teen pregnancy is on the rise. Society is encouraged to aid these girls rather than judge them. Men are not required to be financially responsible unless there is a court order.

What sort of adjustments do newlyweds face?

Would Mary's pregnancy cause more complications?

Friends and townspeople shunned and scorned Mary. Do you think this treatment was fair?

Mary didn't. She knew she was innocent of all their accusations. Would telling people of her special pregnancy have changed anything? For the better or worse?

What are your impressions of Nazareth?

Chapters Six and Seven

Describe Joseph. Is he different than you imagined? How?

*Honestly, Joseph became my favorite character as I wrote this story. My two female beta readers also admitted to finding him admirable. Considering he is rarely mentioned, I may have given him more credit for being a godly man than I should have.

What does the reaction of Joseph's uncle tell you about him? His culture?

*I did my best to picture the birth of Jesus as normal (for the era). His conception was supernatural, but his birth and life was meant to be as normal as any man's.

Who normally visits a woman after she gives birth?

Why do you think God sent the shepherds to see the babe while he was still in the manger?

Would such a visit encourage Mary? Frighten her?

Chapter Eight

As the author, I found this scene in the temple to be pivotal to the path of this story. There was much tradition I didn't truly understand, and couldn't really research, since animal sacrifices are no longer part of Israel's worship. It wasn't until I was working on revisions that I threaded Simeon's prophecy throughout Mary's journal writings.

How is the scene at the temple the same as or different than what you imagined?

Describe Simeon (**Luke 2:25-35**). Why was this devout Jew's reaction to the Messiah so different than what we see from the Sanhedrin during Christ's ministry?

Describe Anna (**Luke 2:36-38**). Do you think it is coincidental that both of these people were older? Does this imply something about older believers?

Which of these encounters would have shaken you more?

Should Joseph have been more assertive or protective of Mary? How so?

Have you ever dwelt on something a person said, as Mary dwells on Simeon's prophecy? Is this a good or bad thing to do?

Chapter Nine and Ten

The scene with the visiting wise men was one of the last ones I wrote. I had difficulty imagining how these men would have acted and how Mary must have felt when they descended on her simple home. **Read Matthew 2:9-11** to see how much the Bible gave me to work with.

Have important people ever dropped in to visit you unannounced? How did it make you feel?

*Note: I didn't say "at home" in this question because most of us are much more likely to experience something like this in a work environment.

What is the most amazing part of the visit?

Would you leave your home, job, and family to protect your children?

How would you have reacted to the news of Herod's murdering spree and death?

*My original draft had several scenes of Joseph and Mary fleeing through Galilee, pursued by the Roman soldiers, facing towns where babies had already been slain. I decided to remove these because they didn't contribute much to the overall plot. Also, Mary learning about Herod's abhorrence after the fact offered up more opportunity for shock value and a human reaction.

Do you believe Mary's reaction was sin?

Chapter Eleven and Twelve

Not much is known about Jesus' childhood. How have you imagined Jesus as a child?

What sort of relationship would a sinless child have with Joseph? Mary? His siblings?

Read Luke 2:42-51. Since becoming a mother (and losing track of my own sons a time or two) I've felt Jesus was a little rebellious and selfish to stay behind in Jerusalem. Of course, we know that can't be true since He never committed sin.

Why do you think Jesus chose to stay in Jerusalem when he was twelve?

Have you ever felt like a failure?

Should this event have prepared Mary for Jesus' eventual departure?

Chapter Thirteen

This scene was added after my beta readers all asked, "What happened to Joseph?" The Bible doesn't give us any information about the years between Jesus at twelve and Jesus at thirty.

Describe your reaction to Joseph's final blessing.

Do you think the tradition of imparting such blessing is positive or negative for the children?

Tradition required the oldest to go first in this situation. Why does Jesus wait until all the others have been blessed?

Chapter Fourteen

The interaction between Mary and Jesus at the marriage feast in Cana has always given me pause. Did she really order the Son of God to help her out of a bind? In reflecting on the actual words in the Bible, I realized that much is left unsaid in this interaction.

Do you think Mary was wrong to ask Jesus to perform a miracle after He told her it wasn't the right time?

Why do you think Jesus changed his mind about helping his mother? Or did he change his mind?

This is the reader's first glimpse at Jesus' disciples. What did you think of them at this meeting?

Chapter Fifteen

Describe Jesus' relationship with his family: Judah, James, Abigail and Mary. Did it change once he left home to begin his ministry?

Do you think Judah's resentment of Jesus is justified? Explain.

*Arranged marriages form another cultural chasm between East and West. However, it was customary in Bible times for one father to enter into a contract with another father or an independent man in regards to a daughter's marriage.

Did you feel better about Abigail's arranged marriage than you did Mary's? Why or why not? What was the difference?

Chapter Sixteen

Judah wants to find fault with everything Jesus does. This leads to an altercation between him and Mary.

Do you feel Mary was right to slap Judah?

Should James have stepped in during this confrontation? If so, should he have sided with Judah or Mary? Why?

*It was difficult for me to have Mary lose control. I've always idolized her and felt she must have been as close to perfect as any human could be. However, when I wrote this scene, she lost control. When I tried to lessen her outburst, it didn't seem like "enough." As a mother, it is difficult when our children disagree.

The weight of what Mary knows about Jesus met with the reality of what people thought of him. Something had to give.

Chapter Seventeen

This interaction in Capernaum seems to justify Judah's scorn for his brother.

How would you feel if your relative treated you like Jesus did his mother and brethren?

Should Mary have been more upset?

Chapter Eighteen

Jesus traveled widely, but he didn't neglect his hometown.

Why did people in Nazareth have a hard time accepting Jesus' teachings and miracles?

Have you found this reluctance true in your own Christian life?

Jesus walked away without a backward glance. Does this

set a precedence for how we should deal with people who are too "familiar" with us to listen to our testimony?

Chapter Nineteen

Women in first century Israel had very few rights and even less independence. Rather than focusing on these restrictions, I wanted readers to consider that Mary would have accepted that cultural norm. However, it wouldn't keep her from feeling the same sort of anxiety we feel as our children age and become independent of us.

Describe Mary's relationship with Judah, Joses, James and Abigail.

Many women traveled with Jesus during his ministry, including Mary's sister, Mary. Why didn't Mary join this following?

Chapter Twenty

This is a mother's worst nightmare: her innocent son is accused of a crime and imprisoned.

Would you have attended Pilate's presentation of Jesus to the crowd?

Were James and Judah wrong to keep Mary from attending?

Chapter Twenty-One

Read the Gospel accounts of Jesus' death: *Matthew 27:31-56*, *Mark 15:20-41*, *Luke 23:33-47* and *John 19:23-37*. Roman crucifixion was a horrible death sentence. It was akin to being tortured to death.

If your son was facing such a death, would you have attended?

Why do you think John was the only male disciple in

attendance (and the Bible is clear that he was in *John 19:25-27*)?

Chapter Twenty-Two

The idea that Mary envisioned her father's Passover lamb overlapping with her picture of Jesus' bleeding body came to me many years before this story was even a flicker at the back of my mind. Something similar happened in a book of Christmas stories told from the perspectives of unnamed people. One of the stories related a shepherd, who had been at the manger, sending lambs to the temple for sacrifice, and then seeing the crucifixion. All of these scenes melded together, giving him an "aha" moment about who Jesus truly was.

What changes is Mary facing during this time?

Do you feel she should have been stronger, especially once she realized the significance of Jesus' death?

What did you think of John during these chapters?

Would Mary have been more or less amazed at the sight of the angels than the other women?

Should Mary have been less surprised by Jesus' resurrection? Why or why not?

Chapter Twenty-Three

Author's note: If you've read the earlier editions, you'll note this is one of two scenes that were added. I just couldn't imagine a devoted son who loved his mother from the cross wouldn't see her after his resurrection. So, I included a short visit when he went to speak to his brother James (which scripture bears out in 1 Corinthians 15:7). After all, something changed that caused his brothers to accept him as the Christ.

What would you have asked Jesus if you saw him after enduring his suffering, death and resurrection?

Chapter Twenty-Four

This is the "next chapter" of Mary's life. I loved pulling the scriptures from her "song" in Luke two into the ending. After all, she had pondered so much in her heart during these many years. I'm sure these words were constantly on the tip of her tongue.

And now that she'd lived to see life after the sword pierced her soul again and again, her praise of God would have so much more meaning. Consider how often you've praised Him in ignorance.

What's different for you when you praise God with full knowledge of pain and suffering?

Would you have ended this story differently? How?

Feel free to send your thoughts on this to info@sharonlee-hughson.com.

Has this story changed your perception of the mother of Christ? How?

What was the most difficult thing Mary faced?

What was Mary's greatest earthly reward?

I hope you enjoyed thinking a little deeper about the events covered in this novel. It makes you a little more like Mary since she "kept all these things, and pondered them in her heart" (Luke 2:19).

For a printable version of this study guide, visit www. sharonleehughson.com/ReflectionsGuide.

FOR TEACHERS

I'm a teacher at heart. I especially love working with teenagers.

Unfortunately, many teenagers don't connect with scripture. Some of this has to do with the digital age wherein they have immediate access to anything and everything they're interested in. And reading scripture takes thoughtfulness which isn't something most young people have to invest.

As a Sunday school and Bible study teacher, I've learned that keeping teenagers engaged in a lesson is a thousand times more difficult than engaging adults. Teens want you to spoon feed them the right answers. They don't want anything to delve into their hearts, and they don't trust most people enough to share what's there anyway.

A Pondering Heart is a perfect book for this age group. Especially for teen girls. The story opens with Mary at thirteen. Although her cultural experience and day-to-day life is nothing like the teenagers of the 21st Century, they can still imagine what it must be like for her.

Or if they don't have the power to imagine it, the words on the page will make them picture it and think about it.

This section will help teacher's or Bible study leaders guide the teenagers in their group to get the most from this study.

Recommendation: Why not start this study at the beginning of December. Aim to hit chapter six and seven around Christmastime.

Lesson Plans

Before you begin reading, ask students what they know about Mary the mother of Jesus Christ. Make a list on a large piece of paper or poster board and post it on the wall for the remainder of the study. Add to it as you learn more things (you may wish to differentiate these with a different color so the students will know what they inferred from God's Word and what they understood during the story's exposition).

DISCUSS: Is it a ton of information? What do they WISH they knew about her?

Explain that you'll be reading a fictionalization of her life over the next few months.

Unlike fiction, which is totally make-believe, a fictionalization uses facts as the starting point for a story. Perhaps they've seen movies "based on actual events." *A Pondering Heart* is the same sort of thing. It is NOT a true story, but it is based on the true story that is told in scripture.

Now have them turn to Luke chapter one. Read verses 26

through 38. Discuss what it might be like to have an angel appear and talk to you. IF you would like to do journaling exercises, provide the students with a notebook and give them five minutes to journal before you read chapters one and two.

JOURNAL PROMPT: Imagine you are Mary. Write the thoughts that are going through your head as the angel appears and then talks to you.

Stop at the asterisks in chapter one. DISCUSS: What do you learn about Mary that might be important later in the story? What do you like about this chapter? What would you change?

After finishing chapter one, DISCUSS: Do you think it was right for Heli to tell Mary to keep this to herself? What do you learn about Mary's relationship with Anna? What do you relate to from this section?

After finishing chapter two, DISCUSS: Do you think it was right for Heli to send Mary to Elisabeth? What do you learn about Elisabeth and Mary's relationship? Do you have an Elisabeth in your life? Who do you talk to when things get confusing?

If there is time, read Luke 1:39-56. DISCUSS: What do you learn about Mary from this passage? What do you learn about Elisabeth? How important is it to have someone "wiser" to talk to about hard and confusing things?

JOURNAL: Imagine you are Mary. Write the thoughts that are going through your head after you see Elisabeth. What are your hopes? Your fears?

Lesson Two

The next lesson should cover chapters three through five.

Before you begin, have students brainstorm what they know about Joseph. Write their responses on a NEW piece of paper or poster board.

DISCUSS: How important is Joseph to God's plan for Jesus?

Read chapter three. DISCUSS: What do you think of the way Heli handled this situation? What do you learn about Joseph?

Now, read Matthew 1:18-25. We don't know if Joseph would have taken Mary as his wife if the angel hadn't appeared to him, but we do know that he had enough faith in God to obey the command when it came to him.

JOURNAL: Imagine you are Joseph. Write what you think when you first learn about Mary's pregnancy and how that changes after your dream from the angel.

READ: Chapter four together. DISCUSS: What are Mary's concerns? Do you think they are realistic? What are Joseph's concerns? What do you learn about them and their faith in God?

READ: Chapter five to the asterisks. DISCUSS: Have you ever been treated unfairly? Ask students to share. Did they respond appropriately? How did it make them FEEL?

READ: Finish chapter five. DISCUSS: We could travel the distance between Nazareth and Bethlehem in a few hours these days. What are some difficulties Mary and Joseph may have faced during their travels?

JOURNAL: Imagine you are a traveler on the road with Mary and Joseph. How would you respond to them? Write an imaginary scene with a conversation between you and them.

Lesson Three

READ: Chapter Six. DISCUSS: What do you think about Joseph's family being the nameless innkeepers? What do you think of them? Do you think they treated Mary and Joseph fairly?

READ: Chapter Seven to the asterisks. DISCUSS: Have you ever witnessed the birth of a baby? What was it like? What do you think it would be like to give birth in a stable full of smelly animals?

READ: The remainder of chapter seven. DISCUSS: Have you ever visited a new mother and baby in the hospital? How is this different? Do strangers usually visit new babies? How do you think Joseph and Mary felt about the shepherds? What do you think of baby Jesus?

READ: Luke 2:1-20. This is a familiar passage, but feel free to discuss it as much as you'd like, highlighting whatever stands out to you in light of the fictionalization.

JOURNAL: Imagine you are a young shepherd boy who was awoken by the chorus of angels. Write your thoughts as you hear their message, travel to Bethlehem and see the baby.

Lesson Four

The next lesson will cover chapters eight through ten.

READ: Chapter eight and Luke 2:22-39. DISCUSS: Why is this an important event in the life of Christ? Why is this an important event in Mary's personal story? How would you feel if a stranger told you "a sword shall pierce through thy own soul"?

The timeline for the next part of the story, as well as the location, is often debated. Let's NOT debate this. I chose a timeline that sent Jesus to Egypt for only a few months, while others have him in Egypt for years before Herod's death.

READ: Chapter nine. DISCUSS: Have you ever hosted strangers in your house? How do you feel when people drop by unannounced? How do you think the people of Nazareth reacted to the strange star and the caravan from the east?

READ: Matthew 2:1-18 and chapter ten. DISCUSS: What do you learn about Joseph and Mary in this chapter? (Add things to their respective charts.) If Jesus really was in Nazareth, why would God send him to Egypt? (Discuss this ONLY if the class brings up the apparent discrepancy. I would LOVE to hear their thoughts, so email them to me if you do have an interesting discussion.)

The book fast-forwards eight years. The next chapter is solely from the author's imagination and added to fill in empty spaces in the storyline, just as chapter thirteen is added to contribute to the WHY of tensions that will grow between Jesus and his brothers.

Lesson Five

READ: Chapter eleven and twelve and Luke 2:40-52.

DISCUSS: What do we learn about Jesus' childhood from these chapters? Do you think it was difficult to have Jesus as a big brother? Why or why not? Have you ever been "forgotten" by your parents? Have students share their experiences. How is this instance in Jesus' life the same and/or different?

READ: Chapter thirteen. No one really knows when or how Joseph died, but he was an important influence for both Jesus and Mary. DISCUSS: What do you learn about

Jesus and his siblings from this chapter? What do you think Mary hoped Jesus might do when they shared their look? Why do you think Jesus waited until last to get his "blessing"?

JOURNAL: Imagine you are one of Jesus' sibling. State who you are and share your thoughts as this final chapter unfolds. How do you feel about Joseph? Mary? Jesus? Your other siblings? What do you think will happen next in your life?

Lesson Six

Now we'll begin the section of the story that includes the three years of Jesus' personal ministry on earth.

READ: John 2:1-11 and Chapter Fourteen. DISCUSS: The Bible leaves many things unstated. How realistic do you feel this retelling is compared to the Bible account? Why do you think that? What do you learn about Mary from this chapter? What do you learn about Jesus? What do you learn about Jewish customs? Do you think it's important to understand Bible customs to "get" the story?

JOURNAL: Imagine you are one of Jesus' disciples. Write down your thoughts about the miracle including any humorous ones you might have before you realize Jesus changed the filthy water into delicious grape juice.

READ: Chapter Fifteen DISCUSS: What is causing tension in Jesus' family? Does this make sense to you? Explain the role of the oldest son in the Middle East. Answer as many questions about the traditions of betrothal contracts as you feel comfortable with. Would you want your parents to decide who you should marry? Why or why not? Try to get them to see the benefits of such an arrangement so it makes sense to them why it was customary.

Lesson Seven

READ: Chapter Sixteen

DISCUSS: The Passover. Review Exodus Why was this an important "family" tradition? Were you surprised by Judah's accusations? Were you more surprised by Mary's outburst? Why?

READ: Chapter Seventeen and Eighteen DISCUSS: Think about YOUR relationship with your mother. How is Mary's relationship with Judah, James, Joses, and Abigail the same or different from yours? How would you describe her as a mother? What did we learn about Jesus' disciples? Has your impression of them changed since the first time you met them? Why or why not? If it has, how?

JOURNAL: Imagine you are either Judah, James or Abigail. Describe how you see Jesus during the events of these chapters. Mention memories or expectations as if he was your older brother and you knew him very well...except, why is he doing all this weird stuff now?

Lesson Eight

This is the end of Christ's life. It can be emotional reading.

READ: Chapters Nineteen through Twenty-One. You may also choose to read portions from Luke 23 and John 19, as you see fit to complement the text.

DISCUSS: Why wasn't Mary at Jesus' trial before Pilate? Do you think this is realistic? Maybe some of them have been in court, discuss how this is nothing like our current justice system. There are no lawyers, just a judge (Pilate) who has ultimate power. Is this a fair system?

DISCUSS: Would you have wanted to be part of the crowd at the crucifixion? Think about the people who are there. Weeping women. Mocking men. Where are the disciples of Jesus? Why is John the only one there? What about the rest of Jesus' family?

JOURNAL: Imagine you are at the crucifixion. What do you see or hear? What stands out to you?

Lesson Nine

READ: Chapter Twenty-Two and Mark 16:1-11.

DISCUSS: Why were the women at the tomb? Who did they see there? How did that change things for the women?

DISCUSS: Have you been to a funeral? What if the dead person sat up in the coffin and started talking? Freaky, huh? Well, up to this point no one had seen Jesus alive. They reacted the same way we would if we heard someone whose funeral we'd attended a few days before was alive.

READ: Chapter Twenty-Three.

DISCUSS: What do we learn about Mary in this chapter? How does her relationship with Jesus change?

JOURNAL: Imagine you are Mary or one of Jesus' siblings. Jesus has been dead a few days but suddenly he appears to you. What are you thinking and feeling? What do you talk to him about?

Lesson Ten

READ: Acts 1:6-14 and Chapter Twenty-Four

DISCUSS: What stands out about the Lord's ascension? How did the final chapter make you feel? Why do you think the author wrote this book?

Review the list of Mary's qualities that you hung up at the beginning of the series. Go over them. Add to the list more of them if you can.

DISCUSS: Why do you think the Bible leaves out more about Mary (and other people) than it tells us? Do you think it's beneficial to read "fiction" books about Bible characters? Why or why not?

JOURNAL: Write a prayer about what you learned from this book. Write a note to the author. Tell her what you liked and didn't like about the book, and if you have other Bible characters who you think would make a good story, tell her that, too.

**Teacher, feel free to email me these letters at info@sharonleehughson.com OR if you want to mail them, send me an email and I'll give you a physical address.

Thanks for sharing Mary's story. God bless you!
Sharon Hughson
Author

MEET THE AUTHOR

Sharon Hughson has long appreciated the power of the written word. For many years, she has written Bible lessons and skits for youth groups and women. Bible characters fascinate her and offer encouragement and insight for real living. But her truest love has always been for reading and writing fiction, and this book marries those passions.

Sharon writes full-time and has decades of experience working with young people in both church and public school, where she works as a substitute teacher. She resides in Oregon with her husband and three cats, and their grown sons and extended family live nearby. In her "free" time, Sharon enjoys playing piano, walking, biking, hiking and traveling with her husband.

This is the first book in her REFLECTIONS series. Although she's published numerous sweet and Christian romances, this series feels like a "new directive" for her writing career.

Visit the Newsletter page **www. sharonhughson.com** to receive updates about new releases. She loves to hear from her readers, and you can use the contact page on her site.

More Books by Sharon Hughson

Sweet Grove Romances

Love's Late Arrival
Love's Little Secrets
Love's Latent Refuge

Texas Homecoming Romances

Love's Lingering Doubts
Love's Returning Hope
Love's Emerging Faith

Nonfiction

Poet Inspired: Revelations and Devotions from Psalm 119
Finding Focus Through the Lens of God's Word

Visit SharonHughson.com for more details!

THE JEWISH CALENDAR

Hebrew	English	Number	Length	Civil Equivalent
נִיסָן	Nissan	1	30 days	March/April
אִיָּיר	Iyar	2	29 days	April-May
סִיוָן	Sivan	3	30 days	May-June
תַּמּוּז	Tammuz	4	29 days	June-July
אָב	Av	5	30 days	July-August
אֱלוּל	Elul	6	29 days	August-Sept.
תִּשְׁרֵי	Tishri	7	30 days	Sept./October
חֶשְׁוָן	Cheshvan	8	29 or 30 days	October-Nov.
כִּסְלֵו	Kislev	9	30 or 29 days	Nov./December
טֵבֵת	Tevet	10	29 days	December-Jan.
שְׁבָט	Shevat	11	30 days	Jan.-February
אֲדָר א	Adar I (leap years only)	12	30 days	February-March
אֲדָר אֲדָר ב	Adar (called Adar Beit in leap years)	12 (13 in leap years)	29 days	February-March

From <http://www.jewfaq.org/calendar.htm>

FOOTNOTES AND SCRIPTURE REFERENCES

1. NAZARETH - CHESVAN

1. i A span is 28.009 cm or roughly 11 inches. This means the cave entrance was slightly more than five feet high.
2. ii Pesach is the Hebrew word for Passover, a holy day observed the fifteenth day of the first month, Nisan, every year.
3. iii Luke 1:28
4. iv Luke 1:28
5. v Luke 1:30
6. vi Luke 1:31
7. vii Luke 1:32
8. viii Luke 1:33
9. ix Luke 1:34
10. x Luke 1:35
11. xi Isaiah 7:14
12. xii Luke 1:35
13. xiii Luke 1:36
14. xiv Luke 1:37
15. xv Luke 1:38

2. HILL COUNTRY

1. xvi Luke 1:42
2. xvii Luke 1:42-43
3. xviii Luke 1:44
4. xix Luke 1:45

4. NAZARETH - ADAR

1. xx Matthew 1:20
2. xxi Matthew 1:21

7. THE BABE - ELUL

1. xxii Luke 2:11
2. xxiii Luke 2:12
3. xxiv Luke 2:14

8. JERUSALEM - TISHREI

1. xxv Luke 2:29
2. xxvi Luke 2:31-32
3. xxvii Luke 2:34
4. xxviii Luke 2:35

12. JERUSALEM - NISAN

1. xxix Luke 2:48
2. xxx Luke 2:49
3. xxxi Luke 2:49

13. NAZARETH - TISHREI

1. xxxii The ancient Hebrew word for tuberculosis used in the Pentateuch.

14. CANA - ADAR

1. xxxiii John 2:3
2. xxxiv John 2:4
3. xxxv John 2:5
4. xxxvi John 2:7
5. xxxvii John 2:8
6. xxxviii John 2:10

16. PESACH - NISAN

1. xxxix Seder is the Hebrew word for the traditional meal served at Passover.

18. NAZARETH - SIVAN

1. xl Mark 6:2
2. xli Mark 6:2
3. xlii Mark 6:3
4. xliii Mark 6:3
5. xliv Mark 6:3
6. xlv Mark 6:4

20. JERUSALEM - NISAN

1. xlvi Luke 19:40
2. xlvii Luke 23:14
3. xlviii Luke 23:15
4. xlix Luke 23:16
5. l Luke 23:18
6. li Matthew 27:22
7. lii Matthew 27:23

21. JERUSALEM - NISAN

1. liii Luke 2
2. liv Luke 23:35
3. lv Luke 23:35
4. lvi Luke 23:34
5. lvii Luke 23:38 This is the King of the Jews.
6. lviii Luke 23:37
7. lix John 19:26
8. lx John 19:26
9. lxi John 19:27
10. lxii Luke 23:44
11. lxiii John 19:28

12. lxiv John 19:30

22. DARK DAYS - NISAN

1. lxv John 1:29
2. lxvi
3. lxvii Luke 24:6
4. lxviii Luke 24:7
5. lxix Mark 16:7

24. JERUSALEM - IYAR

1. lxx Luke 1:49
2. lxxi Luke 1:50
3. lxxii Luke 1:51
4. lxxiii Luke 1:52
5. lxxiv Luke 1:53
6. lxxv Luke 1:53
7. lxxvi John 18:18
8. lxxvii Luke 23:34

Made in the
USA
Lexington, KY